DEADLY BEATING

Reamer had a three-foot length of trace chain in one hand as he advanced on the scout. "You're a dead man, Holten," he snarled.

Wise in the ways of brawlers, Eli Holten said nothing, saving his breath for the contest to come. He backed away from the menace of the whirring links and darted his glance around the area for some form of defense.

That's when he saw the broken ax handle. It would have to do. He faked a dodge in the opposite direction, then ran for the oak shaft.

Reamer anticipated him and the trace chain whistled through the air. Bright splinters of pain radiated from the scout's right forearm as the steel links smashed down on it. Wincing to hold back a cry of agony, Holten jerked his arm away before the sinuous metal links could wrap around and trap him.

Reamer smiled with satisfaction. "I'm gonna like killin' you Holten," he said with a smirk. "I'm gonna like it a lot."

#18
THE SCOUT

REDSKIN THRUST
BY BUCK GENTRY

ZEBRA BOOKS
KENSINGTON PUBLISHING CORP.

Special acknowledgments to Mark K. Roberts.

ZEBRA BOOKS

are published by

Kensington Publishing Corp.
475 Park Avenue South
New York, NY 10016

First printing: May 1985

Printed in the United States of America

*This episode is dedicated to a good friend and fellow Kansan . . . **Bob Gideon**.*

BG

A scout's duties never end. Up before daylight, they are often not in touch with the main column for days at a time. Only the most intrepid of men can be relied upon for this onerous task. To all [of them] who have served under me, I give my most heartfelt thanks.

—Gen. Alfred H. Terry

Out of the ranks of the mountain men, and early-day adventurous explorers came the solid cadre upon which the Civilian Scout Corps was built. Independent, strong, often rowdy, they added a flavor to any command they served.

— The Trailblazers

Chapter 1

Thousands of hoofs struck the prairie, raising a muffled sound like the slow, mournful drum roll at an execution. In a great diaspora, the tribes were on the move. To north, south, east, and west, the vanguard radiated out from the Valley-Where-the-Sky-Fell. The Sioux and the Cheyenne came first and, when they made contact with emissaries of the Pawnee, Crow, Arapaho, and Blackfeet, their people, likewise, joined the aimless migration. For so great a number, they went quietly, these People of the high plains. Heads bowed, shoulders slumped as though in the thrall of a great mystery.

For truly, a mighty omen had been revealed to Kicking Elk and the other dreamers at the immense congregation. Even the powerful and influential Sitting Bull had summoned visions of some momentous event to happen before the time of the next Sun Dance. Black Elk, too, had seen these things.

Soldiers would fall from the sky, wearing wounds given by the Sioux and Cheyenne. That could be told by the markings on the arrows in their chests and backs. All of this would happen at a place where two rivers joined, between tall walls of the soft, white rock. Many of the blue-suits would die and the People would have a great victory. So foretold the dreams of the medicine chiefs. Another remarkable thing happened as well, which lent credence to these prophesies.

The adopted Oglala, Tall Bear, had danced with the *Wiwanyang wacipi*, the Sun Gazers, through the long, hot day of the sacred ritual. His eyesight had not been damaged, though he suffered mightily and bravely showed not a sign of it. He had proven himself *Odakota*, more Sioux than white. Some predicted that he would fight with his Sioux brothers. Others thought he might ride with the pony-soldiers and die with them. All agreed on one thing. It had been interpreted as a sign that the dreams of the *wakanhcapi* would come to pass. None questioned this. None offered different interpretations of the visions.

Thus, traditional enemies became, for a moment, friends as word of these happenings spread among the tribes. Yet, the people went not to their traditional winter homes, to make meat and prepare for the cold months. They wandered far afield, often talking of new dwelling places which they made for themselves in distant, secret places.

"*Wakanya hibu yelo!*" the braves chanted as they journeyed over the rolling ground.

And, truly, each came in a mysterious manner.

With a startled grunt, he bolted upright in the bed.

Tall Bear, *Mahto Tanka* to the Oglala, Eli Holten, chief scout to the Twelfth U.S. Cavalry, came instantly awake, though echoes of his extraordinary and disturbing dreams rebounded in his head. In his nighttime fantasies, the entire Sioux Nation had been on the move. Not alone the *Dakota*, but every tribe on the great plains, the *Palani, Pani, Śahiela, Psa, Mah'piyato,* and *Oyateyamni.* The Arikara, Pawnee, Cheyenne, Crow, Arapaho, and Ponca, his mind supplied the English names. The men and older boys had painted their faces in white, with black lightning-streaked stripes, and went their way chanting that they came in a sacred and mysterious way.

Holten remained rigid, staring into darkness, the whole panoply unreeling on the stage of his mind. A deep conviction overcame him that what he saw was indeed happening. Beside him, a sleek, well-curved form stirred. Constance Albright awakened with a yawn and a stretch.

"You mean — you're ready again?" she asked sleepily.

"Uh — Not. It's nothing. A dream. It woke me up."

"Must have been some dream," Constance remarked as her eager hand explored the region of the scout's naked waist. Her warm, moist fingers encircled a partially erect pillar and kneaded it to firmer life.

"There, you see?" she said tartly. "You really are ready again."

"Uh — Connie — er, that is — ah, what the hell." Eli Holten relented.

The bed was hers, as was the room in the Belle Riviere Hotel in Eagle Pass. The marvelous, wondrously responsive body belonged to the lithe, auburn-haired lovely as well. Eli had met her three days ago.

11

She had come to Eagle Pass to open a millinery store, featuring her own designs and hoping to employ local ladies to do the seamstress work. That the growing community already had a millinery section in its general store had little effect on her plans. Competition, she believed, was healthy for any enterprise. There had been an immediate and intense attraction between her and the tall, hard-muscled, square-jawed army scout.

Holten liked her pluck, he claimed, while his eyes took in her every curve and protrusion with the meticulous evaluation of a successful horse breeder. She thought his occupation "dashing," and praised his courage while she studied his storm-cloud gray eyes and firm jaw, well-proportioned physique and the implied promise of the slight bulge in his loins. Their smiles and admiring glances wrote volumes. By evening of the second day of their acquaintance, they found themselves in bed together. Constance gave Eli's massive organ another playful tweak and pulled aside the sheet that covered them.

"Don't be shy," she said encouragingly. "Ravage me. Tear me apart like the great raging stallion you are."

Holten reached for her. Even her slight weight sent twinges of pain through the slowly healing wounds left by his ordeal in the Sun Dance. Two flaps of skin formed three-sided boxes on his chest, extending some three inches upward from the closed ends near his nipples. The wooden pegs, which had been inserted to hold his rawhide suspension lines, had not hurt so much as the mending process. He would, though, wear the scars proudly for the rest of his days. Holten had been third from last to tear from his tethers and fall in a dreaming stupor only minutes before the afterglow of

12

the Dakota Territory sunset faded into darkness.

He had survived the *wiwanyag waci* ritual of the Sun Dance! Few, if any other, white men could make that claim. This had been the price he had to pay to win the trust and cooperation of Kicking Elk of the Sans Arc in the battle against Captain Breathwaite and his outlaw town of Breakneck Gap. He had met the obligation gladly, though not without considerable trepidation. Now, he accepted the loving attention and tender care of Constance Albright to be only his due.

"That's it — get on top," Eli urged. "I'm — still a little sore, you know."

"Here?" Constance inquired as she touched his injuries. "Or here?" Her hand went to his engorged organ.

"Both places," the scout admitted through a grin. "Though I could go for a lot more pain in the last place."

Swiftly, Constance positioned herself over the supine form of her remarkable lover. She had known few men in her life. The first, at the age of thirteen, had been unexpected, yet not at all unpleasant. She had been seduced by one of her mother's tenants.

A widow, Prudence Albright ran a boarding house in the small town of Avery, Pennsylvania. It proved ample to provide support of her daughter, Constance, and insure her a good schooling. Among her residents was an older man, who worked as an accountant in the excellent forge and steel mill Avery boasted as its major industry. Balding, quiet and mannerly, he had an eye and a passion for younger girls. He had planned his conquest with consummate skill.

On that gray, sodden afternoon, a heavy mist in the sky, Constance remained at home, while her mother journeyed to Pittsburg for the larger staples and new linens for her establishment. Constance had ended her period the previous day and now felt the most delicious and stimulating twinges throughout her body. Her slightest touch brought on shivers of excitement, and she could feel her nipples grow firm and the mysterious juices flow in her secret purse. Sensing this prime of all times, George Coburn moved swiftly toward his goal.

He sat beside Constance in the parlor. Their talk became racy as he used such taboo terms as *leg* and *breast* and *thigh* in describing the fried chicken which had been served at noontime. Constance felt her breath quicken, and her eyes went slightly out of focus, yet she did nothing to discourage him when his hand rested on *her* thigh. It seemed only brief moments before he had the hem of her dress hoisted above her knees and his warm palm lay against the silken skin only inches from the tingling juncture of her legs. She sighed and leaned against him, eagerly anticipating what new, slightly naughty experience they would share.

George cupped her chin with his other hand and leaned down to kiss her. What a strange kiss it was, she thought, as his tongue insistently probed its way into her mouth. And how wonderfully exciting! Without need of coaching, she responded in kind.

The questing hand on her bare thigh rose higher. It slipped under the drawstring of her bloomers.

"Oh! We mustn't do that," Constance cried out as she arrested his movement with both small hands. "Mother says it isn't nice."

"But it is, isn't it? You like the way it feels, don't you?"

Constance sighed again. "Y-yes. It's—terribly good."

Her fingers released their hold, and George edged further downward. He encountered only a few wispy strands of silken hair, which failed to cover even the least part of her swollen mound. At his feathery touch, it began to pulse, and Constance felt a warm and welcome gush as her juices flowed freely. With deft experience, George inserted his middle finger into her cleft, which opened wide to welcome him, and began to stroke her lacy fronds. Constance readjusted her position on the sofa, so she could spread her legs to accommodate this sweet stimulation.

She had often done the same for herself over the past five years, so she saw nothing totally bad in the present arrangement. The results had always thrilled her. But nothing like this! She trembled all over and hoped wildly that he would go even further.

"M-maybe we *shouldn't* do this." She spoke in a tentative whisper. "But it feels so much better than doing it alone."

Aha! He had judged correctly. George clumsily embraced her. "Connie, Connie, you're my own sweet girl," he crooned.

Constance sucked in a sharp gasp of air as George thrust his nimble finger deeper within her purse than she had ever dared try on her own. A jolt of indescribable joy accompanied his penetration. George guided one of her hands to the rigid bulge in his trousers. He fumbled open the buttons of his fly and bade her explore the treasures that waited within.

Constance had done so eagerly. When her soft, damp fingers encircled the fat base of his excited penis, her eyes widened, and she formed a small *oh* of surprise with full, naturally ruby lips. Shaking with the thrill of forbidden joys revealed, Constance withdrew the object of her interest. If possible, her eyes enlarged all the more and her brows nearly collided with her hairline at sight of it.

"Oh—it's—it's so red and so hard." She panted as she squeezed the rigid member close to her barely nubile body.

"Slide it up and down," George encouraged her breathlessly. "It's like—like what I'm doing for you."

More than willing, Constance complied. In some unexplainable manner, it seemed to heighten her own enjoyment. Slowly George straightened out on the couch so that she could continue her ministrations as he lowered his face into the hot, steamy crevice between her tingling thighs.

Constance bit her lip to keep from howling out in furious abandon when his fluttering lips and sinuous tongue replaced his gyrating finger. Wave upon wave of the sheerest enchantment washed over her young body, and she feared she would swoon from such unbridled pleasure.

"Oooooh," she moaned. "We c-can't—we can't be d-d-doing this."

George stopped his magnificent lapping for a moment. "Relax. It isn't hurting you, is it? You do want more, don't you?"

"Oh, yes—yes—only—"

"Do you like my cock?"

"It's—gorgeous. So silky and all, but so hard and hot."

"G-give it a little kiss then, to show how much you appreciate it."

"Y-you mean like we did a little bit ago?"

"That's right. Hurry. I'm burning up."

Constance bent low and placed her tender lips over the broad, flat top of his pulsating organ and began to slather it with her tongue. George sighed in delight and returned to his own ardent activity. How wonderful it tasted. She thrilled. Both sweet and salty. Without need of further instruction, she began to take in more and more. Then she began a gentle, tugging suction that sent ripples of delight through her seducer.

His own pleasure assured, George devoted himself to bringing Constance to her peak. The familiar contractions began, and she redoubled her efforts on George's silken shaft. His tongue found her reactive button, and she went wild until the ultimate exploded over her.

Stripped of her final inhibition, Constance cried out, using a word she had never spoken before, having only heard it from some of the coarser boys at her school.

"Aaaaah, Georgie! Fuck me, Georgie, *fuck me!*"

Making love with Eli Holten reminded Constance of that first, wonderous time. Not that either of them lacked experience. With so large and skilled a hunk of manhood, his frequent visitations to her fountain of joy could be considered an entirely new experience.

She lowered herself now, tingling in anticipation of that first shock of grandness as his plentiful phallus initially parted the folds and began its long slide to the core of her being. She braced her hands on his broad chest and began to swirl her pelvis as she engulfed his ripe, red shaft. Holten moaned and reached out to her, driving her firm, tight buttocks forward as she sank onto his maleness. He groaned in utter abandon at the overwhelming sensations generated by her vise-like grip on his organ.

Slowly, he flexed at the hips and rose to meet her. His unpleasant visions forgotten, he gave himself over entirely to the enjoyment of the moment.

Eli's heart pounded in rhythm with the stirring articulation of their tightly joined loins while his reeling mind gave birth to a succession of new constellations, which glowed brightly in stark whites, lambent blues, and palest zephyrs of rose. His stamina, long since a legend among the amorous ladies of the frontier, matched her own. Holten wondered at their perfect match, as did Constance. Gleefully he began to strain to keep up the pace, oblivious now to the ache in his chest and to their exertions which had opened one side of the lefthand wound.

"Let go, Connie," he urged. "Let it go all the way."

She did and plunged down on his magnificent machine to the hilt. She let go a cry of wild abandon as the blunt shield of his burning tip drove against the rigid dome of her womb, its surging power providing kisses for the pouting mouth of that vessel of life. An electric charge raced through the scout and he surged onward, matching his earlier performances with another virtuoso recital of his varied skills.

Timing became everything, and Eli Holten exerted his utmost to bring them to a howling, surging, mutual completion that set an angelic chorus to singing for them both to hear. Gradually, the peak of sensation declined and, after sighs and gentle touchings, both slipped off into the lesser oblivion of sleep.

Morning brought Eli partial confirmation of his

18

uncanny prescience. The telegraph office sent around a message that reached him at breakfast. His leave had been canceled, and he was to report immediately to Gen. Frank Corrington at Fort Rawlins, Dakota Territory.

It could mean only one thing. General Corrington reserved only the toughest assignments for his chief scout and longtime friend, Eli Holten. It did little to comfort Eli as he prepared to depart.

Only a fast day's ride from Eagle Pass, Eli Holten arrived at the fort an hour before retreat formation the next afternoon. The post seemed unnervingly quiet to the scout. Accustomed to the scurry and bustle of the large military base, his sensitive ears tingled at the sensation of near total silence. Fort Rawlins might be a ghost town, Eli likewise noted. No new assignees sweated and labored under the harsh commands of the troop sergeants. Few of the usual headquarters staff rushed about with sheaves of orders and other papers clutched in their hands. He tied his faithful mount, Sonny, at the rail in front of the headquarters building and entered, casually acknowledging the sentry, who snapped to attention, without saluting, which was proper protocol for a ranking civilian scout.

Inside, the regimental sergeant major ushered Holten immediately into the general's office. Experienced eyes examined the room, seeking the telltale decanter of brandy and open box of cigars. Holten relaxed a little when he saw these accoutrements missing.

"Eli. Good to see you got here so soon. Sorry about the furlough."

"What's the rush, Frank?" Alone, neither man stood

on military courtesy in regard to rank.

"The regiment's been ordered out to support the Ninth and Eleventh. I want you to go along with them." General Corrington held up a restraining hand to keep his chief scout silent. "I know you've been recuperating after that foolish and dangerous display you made of yourself at the Sun Dance. And I'm sure it hurts. The thing is we have to find out what's going on out there."

"How do you mean?" The icy fingers of premonition slid stealthily along Eli Holten's spine.

"The entire Sioux Nation seems to be on the move. A few of our less scurrilous ridge-runners and trappers have brought in reports that sent the other regiments out at once. I need someone I can rely on to scout for this large expedition. We don't want to make the Sioux nervous, or to foment any sort of incident; only learn what's behind all this. To make matters worse, it appears to be not only the Sioux."

"Don't tell me, let me guess," Eli answered back with a tone of sarcasm he hardly felt. "The Cheyenne, Crow, Pawnee, the Arikara, Arapaho, Blackfeet, and Ponca are in on it, too."

"H-how did you know?" Corrington cleared his throat. "At least that's the gist of the reports we've received. Not just here, in this area, but all over the Dakotas. They're not going home, so's to speak. They're—just wandering off in odd directions. That's not all," the general went on as he rose and crossed to the rosewood sideboard.

There he produced the inevitable crystal decanter of brandy and poured two stemmed-footed glasses. "There's some strong rumors filtering down from department headquarters that Gen. Alfred Terry will

20

conduct a major campaign next spring and summer. Its aim will be to round up all hostile and dissident tribes and herd them, once and for all, onto reservations.

"What with all of these people spreading out like a hundred years ago, like in the—how do you say—grandfather times, Terry's sweep could result in a decidedly perilous situation. It could—" Again the general paused while he opened a cedar humidor of his custom Havanas and waved an inviting hand to his chief scout. "It could bring on a bloodbath for civilians and the military alike. To say nothing of the consequences for the Indians." Corrington paused to gulp down his brandy and pour more for both of them.

Yessir. This was going to be one of those piss-cutter assignments, Eli Holten thought, less than slightly amused. Corrington always saved the hard ones for him. He accepted the refill and sipped tentatively.

"So Terry wants us to go find out what's brewing in order for him to feel all safe and comfy down there at Fort Abraham Lincoln."

"Also so he can adequately enlighten the man these headquarters speculators are betting to be leader of Terry's spearhead. Brief him and make sure of proper limitations. Seems everyone is convinced Terry will select the boy general to head up his cavalry screen. Yep—George Armstrong Custer and his Seventh."

"That asshole!" the scout exploded.

"Tut-tut, Eli. I'm aware of your animosity toward Georgie Custer. And—I can't say I blame you. Even so, that's hardly a way to describe a lieutenant colonel in the U.S. Cavalry."

"It serves more than well enough for that particular

21

asshole of a lieutenant colonel." Eli's face had gone hard, his voice grim.

Eli Holten and Frank Corrington had encountered George Armstrong Custer before. It had not been long after the latter's dubious victory at the Washita. At that long-ago conflict, Custer had even brought along the regimental band to play the *Garryowen* while the troopers butchered babes in their mothers' arms. A brutal and senseless massacre of women, children, and old people, informants had described the so-called battle to Eli Holten. One conducted by a sadistic, glory-hungry buffoon. After talking with the self-centered, arrogant, and contemptuous Custer, Holten had to agree. So did his boss, Frank Corrington.

"Fortunately, or perhaps *unfortunately*, Georgie Custer is not in my command," General Corrington summed up as he and his chief scout rode back toward Fort Rawlins from department headquarters in Omaha. "If he was, I'd have him in front of a court-martial so fast for what he did to Black Kettle's people that his balls would still be caught in the crack of his McClellan saddle when the verdict came in."

"If I, or any of my friends in Iron Claw's band of Oglala, got hands on him, there wouldn't be anything to get caught in that crack, general," Eli Holten replied.

Now, in their infinite wisdom, the headquarters heroes saw fit to suggest that George Armstrong Custer might be suited to lead an expedition into country suddenly made full of Indians, of many tribes, both peaceful and hostile, who had taken it upon themselves to wander over the prairie. Yet, it would certainly be in order to find out why and where they intended to go.

Holten rose and downed the last of his brandy. "I'll leave after drawing supplies. Any time the regiment is ready, sir."

"They went into the field half an hour before you arrived. All except Lieutenant Strickland and a patrol that will accompany you. Good luck, Eli. Bring me back what I have to know. Rest assured my best wishes go with you."

"Thank you, general."

"Eli, so far everything has been peaceful. Don't get yourself—or anyone else—killed."

Chapter 2

Hewanzi-Bloka led his family down off the rolling breast of the Earth Mother. Long ago he had learned that safety for a small party traveling the plains lay in not being seen. A wash such as this, thick with tall grass, would provide an excellent place to camp for the night. One-Horn Bull prided himself on being able to care for his wife and three children. Yes! Three, and all alive and healthy. Some men of the Quill Workers' band whom he knew had two or three wives and not so many young who had lived past their first year.

Harsh winters and little food accounted for the death of many of the little ones, as it did for the gray-heads. Weaker than adults in their prime, they wasted away and died. Usually in the Moon of Deep Snows. One-Horn Bull had proven his craftiness by putting aside edible roots and dried buffalo, pemmican made of bear tallow, nuts, and the jerked flesh of elk. Rather than eat their fill each day, as was the wont of most of the

Dakota, he and his family partook sparely, though in sufficient quantity to sustain them. When food grew scarce for others, they still had enough. It had been nearly eleven summers since his first son had been born, and this unusual idea of his had shown its merit many times since. It never occurred to *Hewanźi-Bloka* that following one of his time-tested dictums — to make a hidden camp in strange country — could lead to disaster.

Only a few seconds after entering the arroyo, a huge, hairy-faced white man rose out of the waving buffalo grass, a rifle already to his shoulder. Flame blossomed at the muzzle and a fat .56 caliber slug sped toward One-Horn Bull's chest.

"It worked like you said, Myron!" the shaggy apparition shouted in triumph as he opened the breech of his Sharps.

By then *Hewanźi-Bloka* lay writhing on the ground.

More spurts of yellow-orange appeared in the grass, spread in a deadly arc across the pathway chosen by the cautious Oglala warrior. His trail to safety had become a deadly ambush.

"Kill them redstick bastards!" another white yelled. *Makaciqa,* One-Horn Bull's ten-year-old son, managed to break the grip of surprise paralysis and nock an arrow to his small rabbit bow. The shaft sped true and buried half its length in the chest of the white man who had killed his father. The outlaw grunted and grasped at the shaft, tugging stoutly on it until the chipped flint tip sliced through his aorta and all strength left him. An incredulous look crossed his wide, gap-toothed face a moment before he fell dead at the feet of the Oglala he had murdered.

A moment later, three slugs ripped Little Skunk's belly apart. His younger brother howled in fright, though he kept his head and tried to grab up the dangling reins of his older sister's pony and lead her away from the danger. His effort, though courageous, netted little.

"Hey, Myron, that li'l fart's tryin' to get away."

"I see him."

The tall, lean man who led this collection of border ruffians rose from where he knelt and took aim on the fleeing seven-year-old's back. His .50/70 Remington Rolling Block carbine roared in the narrow confines of the draw as it belched fire, lead, and smoke. A small, scarlet flower bloomed between the lad's shoulder blades, and he snapped forward, to somersault over his pony's blocky head. A fraction of a second later the meaty smack of the impact reached the ambushers' ears.

"Grab that woman!" Myron Henshaw commanded.

"An' the girl," one of his followers chortled gleefully.

"Hell," another protested, "she ain't more'n nine or so."

"She'll do," a third killer declared hungrily.

White Fawn began to scream as the two men dragged her off her mount. She kicked and flailed with her short riding quirt, though she did little damage. Rough hands clasped her body and eager fingers clawed at her elkhide dress.

"Ow! She's some hellcat, for certain sure," the assailant on her left bawled.

Off to the side, three men had surrounded White Fawn's mother. *Anpetuwiwin* held a long-bladed knife in one hand, which she used to slash at the white men

26

around her. One reached out for her leg, and she swung with a vicious backhand swipe. The keen edge of the Green River trade knife opened his palm to the bone.

"Christ! Somebody help us here, huh? The bitch cut me good."

Only the briefest of smiles lit Day-sun Woman's lips as she lashed out with one foot to kick another would-be rapist under the chin. His teeth clicked together, and one rotten, yellowed husk flew from his mouth.

"You stinking cunt!" he growled and dived forward, strong, raspy fingers closing around *Anpetuwiwin's* ankle.

Another of the frontier scum leaped from a rock in the sidewall of the draw and wrapped his arms around her chest, pinning her arms to her sides. A swift moment later, he howled in agony as Day-sun Woman whipped her right forearm up to the left and buried the point of her skinning knife in the muscle behind his left wrist. The tip went between the bones and protruded below.

Groaning with agony, he fell away, to be kicked into unconsciousness by the Sioux woman's prancing horse.

"Get her, goddamnit!" Henshaw growled. "What's the matter? Three of you can't corral one tiny squaw?"

"You come here and give it a try, Myron," Bart Tanner complained.

Myron crossed the sandy bottom of the wash and swung the thick barrel of his Remington rifle. He gauged his blow so that it did not drive the Oglala women into unconsciousness. Groggy, her head buzzing with numbness and a dull ache, *Anpetuwiwin* swayed in the high-backed, wooden saddle and fell to the ground. Instantly, the four men gathered around her. One reached for the hem of her soft, pliable elkhide dress. A high, thin shriek of pure rage split the air around their ears, and the aroused men took time to look toward the source.

White Fawn lay naked on the sandy bed of the wash. One of the hardcases had his drawers down and a thick, reddened lance protruded from his crotch. This he stroked gently as he eyed the little Sioux girl's slender, bronze body. Her flat chest stimulated him wildly, as did the soft, rounded belly, sunken now by her supine position. His gaze was drawn over and over to the small, chubby mound which she struggled to keep protected with her crossed legs. Completely hairless, its tender slit beckoned unbearably to the youthful outlaw. He'd always had a hanker for younger girls, since the age of twelve, when a precocious eight-year-old had been his first conquest. He sank to his knees and grasped her ankles.

With a powerful wrench, he yanked her legs apart and scuffled forward. "This is gonna be *some* fun," he enthused to his companion.

"Yeah, Lenny. Hurry up, though. I want my turn."

"You'll get it, Buell."

Lenny squirmed lower and closer, until the hot tip of his engorged organ brushed against White Fawn's fevered flesh. With one hand, Lenny rubbed his tingling device in the tightly pinched crevice that refused to cooperate. He reached out swiftly and slapped White Fawn on her right cheek.

"Help me a little, baby."

A wail of utter anguish tore from White Fawn's throat as Lenny pried her small cleft open with rough fingers. With a grunt of effort, he drove some three inches of his throbbing shaft into her dry passage. Blood flowed and the little girl screamed in pain and horror. A dozen feet away, her mother fared little better.

Three men had to hold Day-sun Woman down on the ground, while a fourth readied himself to force his will upon her. A long, slim member swayed before her eyes and her attacker knelt astride her. He lowered his dripping maleness toward her face and wiggled it in a tight circle.

"Suck it, sweetie. Suck it real good."

Anpetuwiwin spat at him and tried to buck him off. The next instant, she exploded inside with fiery misery.

For a moment she thought she had been pierced by an iron rod. A look between the wide-spread legs of the man on her chest showed her another lust-filled face. The unshaven, powder-grimed beast continued to rut on her, a thin trickle of spittal running down his chin as he lost himself in concupiscence. Waves of sickness, shame, and rage washed over Day-sun Woman as she endured the indignity and torment of her violation.

Ever so quickly, or so it seemed, the ugly creature began to pant brokenly and then lunged against her, quivering while he squealed like a pig. Swiftly, another of the murderers took his place. *Anpetuwiwin* closed her eyes and her mind to her humiliation and misery. Only the shrieks and moans of her ravished daughter haunted the empty corridors of her brain.

The raping went on for a long time. When it ended, mother and daughter lay dead and bloodied on the bare earth.

Discontent had not become the sole province of the tribes from the high plains. Five soldiers, led by Trooper Howard Barryman, felt the sting of disaffection. The army, they knew, was their enemy. Like fighting men from the beginning of time, they believed an enemy existed for the purpose of looting. Under Barryman's tutelage, Vince Liscomb, Butler Bell, Toby Whitter, and Neal Thorne managed to strip the army of a great deal.

"Put it this way," Barryman had explained to them some two months previously when he first came to Fort Rawlins. "Blankets, stretchers, medical alcohol, food, saddles, and tack, damned near anything the army has in large quantities, can be turned into cash money on the frontier."

"We been sneakin' off some ammunition and blankets from time to time," Toby Whitter admitted.

"Hell, that's nothin'," Howard Barryman responded. "If you're gonna steal, steal big. What I got in mind . . . but I'll tell you about that when the time comes. What say we work together and see what can be done?"

They accomplished an astonishing amount.

Now, with the first passes in the same two months clutched firmly in their hands, the quintet set out for the large cache they had deposited some five miles from the fort. They would rig travois and haul all of the stolen items they could handle to a meeting with their civilian contact, then on to Eagle Pass for some serious drinking. Behind them they left two highly concerned persons discussing the fruits of their labor.

Blue eyes burned with an intensity out of the craggy face of Gen. Frank Corrington as he sat behind his desk in the regimental headquarters of the Twelfth U.S.

Cavalry at Fort Rawlins. His square jaw had a pugnacious set to it as he listened to his adjutant tick off items on a list.

"Twenty-eight blankets, seven hundred rounds of forty-five-seventy ammunition, two Springfield carbines, five bayonetes, eleven iron cook pots, nine complete sets of halters, bits, and reins, six—if you can believe it—McClellan saddles, one rifle boot, a gallon of medical alcohol. That completes the list, general."

"*For this month only?*" Frank Corrington shot back, heavily emphasizing each word.

"Uh—yes, sir. This month. Added to the other losses, we have enough missing gear to outfit an entire troop and get them drunk for a weekend."

"It's not funny, Abner."

The adjutant sobered. "No, sir. Of course not, sir. It's only—well, we've been losing entirely too much for it to be an accident. Likewise, pilferage is never this severe. The men know better."

"Do they? This—ah, pilferage you refer to—could it be outright theft for a profit?"

"Someone *selling* the stolen goods to another party? Who, sir?" Abner Styles inquired with avid curiousity.

"That's something we do not know. What's the quartermaster think of this?"

"Basically what you said just now. Someone is deliberately stealing certain items. Things with a cash value on the frontier."

"Newly assigned men are the first, obvious suspects," the general mused aloud. "Whoever it is has to be clever about it. What has been taken fits the theory that this is being done for a profit. With three regiments in the field, it should be easy to catch whomever

31

it is. Provided, of course, that he isn't out chasing Indians. Tighten things up, Abner. Plug every leak. Put a sentry in the quartermaster stores at night, if necessary. I want this thievery stopped."

"When we gonna stop all this?" Neal Thorne asked Howard Barryman.

"Now's not the right time," the leader replied.

"Look, Howard, we've damned near looted that building dry. Officers might be stupid, but they're gonna catch on to this one of these days. We get caught and you can be sure it'll be more'n stockade time. We'll be in Leavenworth."

"Getting scared?" Howard sneered.

"N-no," Neal answered defensively. "Only—"

"Only, shit! Listen to me. We've got a big score just waitin' for the right time. After that, we can kiss the army good-bye and haul our asses outta here. You stick with me and you'll be a rich man some day."

"Oh? How's that?" Toby Whitter demanded. He stretched his young, gangly body and scratched at a louse in his straw-colored hair.

"It's—something big. I can't tell you all about it now." The truth was, Howard didn't know the exact details. He had only been told to be ready to steal the army blind when the word came. He'd not argue the point with a pair of numb-brains like Whitter and Thorne.

Wet behind the ears punks, he considered them, who had come in as part of the last replacement column. Hell, they hardly knew how to stay on their horses as yet. Of the two, Howard considered, Thorne had the most promise. Stringy muscled, with a rat face and shifty brown eyes, he looked like the guttersnipe he admitted to being. Some whore's woods' colt, no doubt, dumped out to fend for himself in New York's tough Hell's Kitchen district. But it had made him wise in the ways of things. That Howard appreciated.

"Anyone for a little five card stud?" Butler Bell inquired.

"Naw. That's fer rich assholes with more money than brains," Neal Thorne replied. " 'Sides, that buyer should ought to be here soon. When's he comin', Howard?"

"Should have been here by now. I'm tellin' ya, boys, this is only goober pea money compared to what comes in a little while."

A wagon rattled outside the small shack the thieves had discovered in a wide, deep wash outside the fort. The sound drew nearer and soon a man's voice could be heard halting his team. Footsteps pounded on the hard ground, and solid knuckles rapped the door.

"It's open," Barryman growled.

A squat, beefy-faced individual entered. He wore an expensive eastern-style suit and bowler hat on his round head. Small ears, nearly a match for the cup-handle appendages of Howard Barryman, protruded from below a fringe of graying hair. Their owner rubbed fat, pink hands together in anticipation and helped himself to three fingers of whiskey without being invited.

"Well, well, what do you have for me this time?" he inquired.

After the transaction had been completed, the conspirators rode on to Eagle Pass. Flush with a great deal more money than their meager thirteen dollars a month pay, they sported lavishly among the fragrant lillies of the Thunder Saloon, consuming champagne and steaks, huge quantities of sherbet, and paying five dollars a trick to go upstairs and have their ashes hauled. All five suffered hangovers when they started the long day's journey back to Fort Rawlins. Each brought along several bottles to ease their travels and for security against the boredom of life on the post.

They arrived to find their names on the duty roster for nighttime sentries. Howard Barrymen endured it with stoic silence, while Toby Whitter and Neal Thorne complained bitterly, like spoiled children. Butler Bell scowled and accepted his rotten fate. Vince Liscomb declared it to be a plot of the elitist officer class.

On their second night of guard watch, Toby and Neal secreted a bottle of whiskey out in the nearly empty stable. They made frequent trips there, deviating from their appointed rounds to do so. It didn't take long for the inexperienced youngsters to become thoroughly intoxicated. As a result, they wound up seeking the elixir of John Barleycorn at the same time.

"Huh! Wha' you doin' here, Nealie-weelie?" Toby slurred.

"T'same as — as y-you're doin', Toby-woby. I'sh gettin' drunk."

Thorne tipped back the bottle and took a long pull.

"Cut tha' out. I ain't got any for me."

"Thersh more — uh — here."

Toby drank and belched. He and his partner in crime leaned from the effects of the heavy weather they

34

had taken aboard. They leaned forward so far their shoulders touched. Neither of them remained in any condition to hear the stealthy approach of the sergeant of the guard.

"Well, well, me buckoes. What have we here? Ye two darlin' lads out here pullin' off each other's tallywhackers? What a cozy scene that is."

Toby jerked erect so abruptly he staggered backward and would have fallen, except for the corral rail. "Unh! N-no, sergeant. We—we wasn't doin' nothing' like tha'."

Sergeant Malloy sniffed suspiciously. "Sure an' do I not smell a wee drop o' spirits about the air?"

"Spir—spirits? Uh, no. Not around here. Don' smell a thin'," Neal muttered.

"Of course ye can't, ye bein' so soaked in the swill y'er like the pig farmer who fell in the sty. Ya dumb, bleedin' jackasses! Y'er drunk on duty, that's what ye are. I'll be havin' yer guts far garters an' yer asses fer apple sauce fer this! Come to attention, the both of ye. Shoulder arms! Forward march! It's to the guardhouse I'm takin' ye. In the marnin', I'll be makin' me report to the regimental sergeant major and to himself, the general, considerin' the darlin' colonel is out with the boys. Won't surprise me to find yer names on a roster of court-martial."

Toby sobered faster than Neal. He looked at his friend with shocked, puzzled eyes. "Oh—shit," he moaned.

Chapter 3

"Under the authority granted me by the Department of Dakota, the Department of the Army and the War Department, I hereby convene this court-martial and declare it in session." General Corrington lowered the paper in his hand and looked around the room at the officers and enlisted men standing rigidly at attention. A table had been provided for the two accused and their counsel, a young lieutenant fresh from officer's cavalry training. Across from him, at an equally small podium, stood Major Beersman, the quartermaster. All seemed in order.

"You may be seated," the general commanded. "The officers of the court having been properly sworn, we are ready to hear testimony. Are you prepared to proceed, Major Beersman?"

"Yes, sir. My first witness is Corp. Faine Hinton."

"Corporal Hinton, take the stand," the regimental sergeant major, acting as bailiff, called out.

When the young NCO had responded to the summons, the RSM approached and extended a Bible. Hinton raised his right hand, placed the left on the book, and repeated the oath.

"Now, corporal," Major Beersman began. "Let us return to the night of the fifteenth, just two days ago. What was your regular duty assignment on the fifteenth?"

"I was corporal of the guard, sir."

"Were you on duty following retreat formation that day?"

"Yes, sir. I had the usual twenty-four on and twenty-four off schedule, sir."

"I'll draw your attention to the accused. Are you acquainted with Troopers Whitter and Thorne?"

"Yes, sir. They are both in C Troop of the Twelfth."

"On the day in question, do you know what their duties consisted of?"

"Oh, yes, sir. They was, er, were both on guard-mount."

"So then, under your direct supervision, is that correct?"

"Yes, sir. Me an' Sergeant Malloy. He was sergeant of the guard."

"Who had OOD for that day, do you recall?"

"Yes, sir. Lieutenant Daniforth, sir."

"Thank you, corporal. Now, returning to the fifteenth, in the hours after retreat formation. Did you have occasion to observe the activities of either Trooper Whitter or Trooper Thorne?"

"Yes, sir. Both of them at one time or another."

"Please enlarge, if you will."

"They had separate guard posts. Both walking patrol, sir. One had the stable and corral area, that was Trooper Whitter, and the other the west wall."

"Go on."

"I made my usual checks, every half hour, sir, until ten at night, then we take turns every two hours, like the sentries—two on and two off—so's we can get some sleep. Anyway, sir, I went past Whitter and Thorne some ten times up until lights out."

"How would you describe them?"

"Sir," the defense counsel exclaimed, "I object, sir."

Frank Corrington leaned forward. "Oh? On what grounds?"

"Begging the general's pardon, sir, but this corporal is not qualified to diagnose persons or to determine their well-being."

"I don't think the judge advocate intended this to be a medical determination, lieutenant. I'll overrule that so we can go on."

"I'll restate my question," Major Beersman offered. "On those occasions when you inspected their posts, how would you describe the appearance, response, and deportment of Troopers Whitter and Thorne?"

"They seemed right enough, sir," Corporal Hinton replied. "They challenged in the proper manner. Correctly answered my questions about various of the general orders for sentries."

"What about later?"

"Uh—well, sir, that's when things started to go down hill, so's to speak."

"How do you mean, 'down hill'?"

"Long about midnight, they started getting sloppy. Both Whitter an' Thorne, that is, sir. Came on Whitter at the eleven o'clock check and he didn't even challenge the person on his post. Chewed him for it a bit and went on. He went off duty for two hours then, like I did. Next shift, when I posted the men, Trooper Whitter slurred his words a bit and couldn't pronounce 'military' in 'Walk my post in a military manner.' That time, too, at one o'clock in the morning, sir, I thought I smelled whiskey on Trooper Thorne's breath."

"I see. Thank you, corporal. What did you do accordingly?"

"I reported my suspicions to Tim Malloy, uh, the sergeant of the guard, sir."

"And what did he do?"

"Objection."

"Do you know what he did?"

"Yes, sir. He roused some sleeping sentries and told them and me to come along with him."

"What did you find when the sergeant visited the two posts?"

"Nothing, sir."

"Nothing?"

"That's right, sir. Both of them were absent from their posts."

"That is a grave offense, isn't it, corporal?"

"It certainly is, sir."

"Did you subsequently locate the missing sentries, Troopers Whitter and Thorne?"

"Yes, sir. At the stable. They was, ah, drinkin' a little whiskey."

"Whiskey?"

"Yes, sir. Right from the bottle."

"Thank you, corporal. I have no further questions."

"Cross examine?" General Corrington inquired.

The young lieutenant sat slump-shouldered between

the defendants. "No questions, sir."

"Call the next witness," Corrington, as president of the court, declared.

"Sergeant Malloy."

"It's not going good," Howard Barryman admitted to his cohorts.

"Not good, hell," Butler Bell snapped back. "That fat bastard Corrington's got them all measured and fit for a noose. Shit, even if they don't get the firing squad or the gallows, they'll never see the outside of Leavenworth again."

"So long as they don't try to use our little, ah, business undertaking as a deal to get a lighter sentence," Barryman speculated aloud.

"They won't," Vince Liscomb stated flatly. His weak, waterly, hazel eyes glittered with innate intelligence and the fierceness of a zealot. An unruly mop of black hair flopped over the left side of his forehead, and he reached to stroke it in an unconscious gesture.

"How are you so sure?" Bell asked.

"You've made believers out of 'em, Howard," Liscomb explained, addressing Barryman instead of his interrogator. "They worship the ground you walk on. I wish there were some way to get them out of this, though. Stupid to drink on duty like that."

"They're kids," Barryman interceded for the accused members of his theft ring. "Why, Whitter's only twenty, Thorne, twenty-two. Hardly dry behind the ears. But, you know, we might be able to use this to our advantage. I mean, the men in garrison now don't much like this speedy court-martial and the possible punishment that might be given out. Maybe we can use that to help us make the big score I told you about."

Hotter fires flared behind the thick lenses of Liscomb's spectacles. "Yeah. Like bringing on the overthrow of the decadent officer class. A revolution. Sure, that's the thing."

"What's he talkin' about?" Bell crabbed.

"Liberate the masses!" Liscomb shouted. "Free the oppressed workers! Destroy the petit bourgeois. Bring about the millenium! Power to the people!"

Barryman made a face, disliking Liscomb's rhetoric because he distrusted all zealots. Even so, he marked well the words and the rumbling tone of power that colored Vince's diatribe. Maybe the idea wasn't all that bad after all. He'd have Vince try that out on some of the disaffected soldiers here at Rawlins.

They had made good time. Eli Holten appreciated the benefit of working with an experienced frontier officer like Thad Strickland. The large patrol had covered considerable ground at a faster than usual pace. Strickland cantered the horses for half an hour, trotted them for the same length of time, then walked, dismounted, for fifteen minutes. "Forty miles a day on beans and hay," was not just a line in a song to the young lieutenant.

"Not an Indian yet?" Strickland remarked when Eli returned to the column shortly after noon.

"No. But they could be anywhere. Even if they're not trying to hide from us, we've no idea which direction some of the bands took, nor how many are traveling together."

41

"You were at that Sun Dance, right? That should have given you some idea when the affair broke up."

"Uh, Thad, I wasn't exactly all that coherent after the Sun Gazing. Fact is, I went out of there on a travois. Some of Kicking Elk's warrior society took me to Eagle Pass. It was three days after that before I even answered to my name."

"God. I've heard stories over the years, of course. Thought a lot of it was exaggerated. Is it really that difficult?"

"And more," the scout assured him. "Some braves die of the dancing, or go blind from staring at the sun for a whole day. Often one or more of the boys of eleven or twelve who are dancing for the first time, to enter the *Wambli Wacipi*—the Eagle Dancers' lodge of the Sun Dance—die from dehydration after a day without liquids and all that exposure. It happened when I danced at seventeen and I've seen it since. I was lucky."

"Hummm. I, for one, am willing to forego all that. What say we swing a bit further south? If you've not seen any tracks . . ." Strickland let it hang there.

"Oh, I've seen tracks. Old ones, some ridden over by shod hoofs, nothing fresh enough for us to hope to catch up."

"Isn't that going to be the whole story?" the youthful-looking officer asked ruefully.

Holten snorted. "I'd say so. Hell, it's been more than a week. But the power-that-be at headquarters decrees, and we can only go along with it."

An hour later, Eli topped a rise and saw one of the most spectacular panoplies of the high plains.

Spread out in a long, slowly moving column, some thirty lodges of Sioux were on the move. Except for the ponies of the warrior society chosen as that day's route guards, and their remuda of fresh mounts, every horse had a travois and a passenger. Married women, some with babes in cradle boards, rode astride the beasts. Some of the travois carried heavy, dun-colored bundles and clusters of slender pine poles, which marked the tipis of the moving village.

Others were laden with household goods, the elderly and infirm, or small children. Older boys and girls frisked about between the legs of the striving animals or walked, holding hands, with the single women and girls at the rear of the procession. The *akicita* galloped along the flanks and ranged out ahead.

Others, Holten knew, would be several miles behind, making their back trail secure. All wore their brightest, most festive clothing. A miasma of dust hovered over the caravan, rising high into the once still air. The scout noted one remarkable difference.

Rather than the shrill shouts of youngsters at play, the melodious singing of the young, unmarried women and the barbed jests shouted by the route guards, there came a marked silence, relieved only by a low-cadenced drone.

"Make way! In a mysterious manner I come!" every brave chanted, the sense of their words rising to Holten's ears, somewhat distorted by distance and the steady thud of hoofs.

Eli wheeled his horse and galloped back to the short file of troopers. His smooth, sun-browned forehead wrinkled with deep lines as he ruminated on the meaning of this phenomenon.

"I found you some Indians," the scout announced as he rode up to Lieutenant Strickland.

"Amazing. I'd grown convinced all we'd collect would be saddle sores. How many?"

"A hundred, hundred and ten. Thirty lodges. An entire village on the move. They're Oglala and headed the wrong way."

"Let's go talk to them," the officer suggested.

"My idea, too," Holten offered with a fleeting smile.

Long before the arrival of the thirty-five cavalrymen, the camp police had sighted their approach. When the soldiers trotted down the long slope to the route of march, in column of twos, the moving village had drawn close in a compact, defensive position. Looks of bemused speculation and expressions of confusion went the rounds of hawk-beaked bronze faces when Lieutenant Strickland displayed a large square of white handkerchief on the tip of his sabre to indicate they came in peace. The leader of the *Cante Tinza*—Brave Heart society—and two of his clubmen rode out to greet the white men.

"We come in peace," Holten told them in Lakota.

"I know you," came the reply.

Holten smiled. "You should, *Lowansa*. I danced beside you in the *wiwanyag wacipi*."

Singer reached out and they clasped forearms in friendly greeting. His smile showed a plethora of large, even white teeth. "You are welcome, Tall Bear. These soldiers are not."

"Oh? Why is that?"

"We are on a sacred mission and we are late."

"Really? Can you tell me about it?"

"Yes. *You* I can tell." Singer made it clear that the cavalry troopers were not to be made privy to his story.

"Like you, it took me a long while, more than six

44

suns, to recover after the dancing. My brother, Gray Beaver, is civil chief of our band, and he decided all would wait until I could ride again. That is why we are late. You learned of the prophesies from the medicine chiefs? The great power awakened by the Sun Dance?"

"No. Kicking Elk took me to the white man lodges called Eagle Pass. I still lay in spirit dreams of my own at the time. So I have heard nothing."

Swiftly, though in exacting detail, *Lowansa* told Holten about the visions of soldiers falling out of the sky, killed by Sioux arrows and of the greater mystery of this mighty battle being fought in some distant place. After he described the location, the Oglala warrior paused. Holten frowned.

"There is such a place, much like what you describe. It is far to the west of here in the land the white men call Montana. Is that why you are traveling such a distance from your usual winter camp place?"

"No. We go as messengers, all of the People do, to spread the story of this powerful medicine to all tribes. To invite them to put aside old grievances and join the *Dakota* and the *Śahiela* in the final great battle that will drive these," Singer said, casting a scathing, contemptuous look at Lieutenant Strickland and the cavalrymen, "unwelcome ones from our land for all time. It was speculated by some, including your father, Iron Claw, that Tall Bear would join his people in this fight."

Lowansa paused and studied Eli Holten with a scowl. "Others say that when that time comes, you will be with the pony-soldiers and that you will die as a white man, not live as a *Dakota*. Which shall it be?"

Holten had to consider this a while. Upon how he answered hinged the success of their mission to turn back the wandering tribes. He passed a hand over his face, to wipe away a sheen of accumulated perspiration and to rearrange his features. As he began to speak, he made the sign to indicate that what he said was the truth.

"It is not given for any mere man to know these things. I would ask the medicine chief, Sitting Bull. Or talk to Crazy Horse before I could know what is deep in my heart. When is this to be?"

"Before the next Sun Dance."

"A year away," Holten mused aloud. Suddenly he recalled the rumors General Corrington had related to him.

If Terry set out in the spring, especially if he allowed George Custer to lead his spearhead, then some sort of pitched battle would be the result, Custer could always be counted on to whip up a fight. He had also heard speculation that the Democratic Party intended to put forward Custer as a candidate for president. They had made a few equally bad choices in the past and probably would again, in the future. If the arrogant and flambuoyant Custer had political ambitions, he would damned sure stir up a glory-showered Indian campaign. One in which a lot of Indians got suddenly dead.

Of course, Holten thought bitterly, if he could arrange it, Custer would prefer to ambush a peaceful, unsuspecting village. Preferably one from which the warriors had gone elsewhere to hunt or make medicine. Had Terry and his superiors also learned of this strange prediction? Surely they would not seriously undertake a roundup of off-reservation Indians, like the one proposed, in light of it. At last he ordered his soaring speculation and made more complete reply.

"I serve the pony-soldiers, *Lowansa*. I must do their bidding in these things. If, in my heart, I find that I should put my lot with my *Dakota* brothers, then it shall be as those people say. I will fight if I must. If the soldiers are obeyed now, though, it is possible to avoid this dream battle, to live in peace."

"How do you say this? All whites are *kiyuksa*. *They* break their own customs by coming into our land when the marks-on-paper say they cannot. *They* break their own customs by killing the People for no cause. *O'ko wapi!* If you trust the white men, sooner or later, *onze nihupi kte lo*."

To the Indian way of thinking, most whites seemed to speak nonsense; that Holten would allow. That one inevitably got screwed in the ass by them, figuratively or literally, he did not believe. How then, could he convince his Oglala brother?

"All the soldiers want is for your band to return to your usual wintering grounds. They will send men to escort you to see no harm comes to your people. They are not angry. They do not wish to harm you. This is not punishment. Like in the battle in the Valley-Where-the-Sky-Fell, the soldiers are on the side of the *Dakota*."

"You must talk of this with Gray Beaver. He is chief of the *Wipatapi*."

That accomplished even less, as Holten talked earnestly and translated for Lieutenant Strickland. What he had told Singer, and later to Gray Beaver, was not strictly true. If the migrating Sioux and Cheyenne would not return to their proper locale, punitive measures were authorized by headquarters. Holten had felt

47

it prudent to omit this from his explanation. Even with the edited version, the civil chief of the Quill Workers' band remained adamant.

"We must carry the word. It is a part of the dream medicine. All must obey. I have spoken."

That ended that. Eli Holten shrugged, explained to Thaddeus Strickland, and they departed to rejoin the troops. Before they reached the waiting column, the Sioux began to march again.

"What do we do now?"

"Thad, it's refreshing to work with someone who will ask that question in the beginning, rather than when we're up to our asses in howling hostiles. The way I see it, there isn't a hell of a lot we can do. These scattered bands are bound to gather with more as time goes on. We might as well shadow them and see that nothing happens to break the peace on either side."

"Well — that is in the scope of my orders. I suppose it will do no harm."

Eli started to make a reply, only to be interrupted by a soft moan from behind a thick screen of willow branches. He and the lieutenant dismounted and walked in that direction.

"What in hell is that, do you suppose?" Strickland inquired of his scout.

"Sounded human. We'll see soon enough, I imagine. I only hope — "

"What?" The officer's question sounded hesitant.

"I hope it's not what I suspect it to be."

The scout reached out and parted the leafy branches.

"Oh, hell, it is," Eli exploded.

On an elkhide blanket, a young Sioux girl lay, her

48

dress hiked to her buttocks, legs widespread, her swollen belly heaving with each painful contraction. She couldn't be a day over sixteen, Eli Holten estimated. Stolen away from the migrating village, a custom demanded, to deliver her child.

"Why, she's about to have a baby," Thad Strickland blurted.

"How right are you are."

"I — this is all strange to me," the officer stammered. "But it looks like she needs help. Her face is swollen and discolored. She seems to be in a lot of pain for what she's experiencing. I — I guess you'll have to do it, Eli."

"Me? I don't know anything about delivering a baby."

Chapter 4

The Sioux girl screamed again. A stunned Eli Holten dropped to his knees beside her.

A gush of thick, red-streaked fluid issued from her distended vagina.

"Her water broke," Strickland said wonderingly.

"Now what?" Eli pleaded.

"We just wait, I suppose. Uh—ask her how far apart the contractions are."

Holten did, using his facility with the *Lakota* language. "She says about three minutes."

"Anytime now. Can you get her to spread her legs a little more?"

She complied, moaning all the while. Then another shriek split the hot afternoon. Holten maneuvered himself between her legs. She began to make feeble waving gestures and murmured harsh, excited words.

"She says we have to get away. To go. It is unclean for men to be present at a time like this."

"But she's in terrible pain," the lieutenant protested. "She says—oh, shit! Look at that."

Holten pointed to the girl's dialated opening, where a second, deep red cleft had appeared. "It's a breach birth, like a horse sometimes," the scout announced. "We have to stay now." Quickly he explained to the panting, wide-eyed girl. She started to protest, then broke off in another howl of agony.

"Can—can you, uh, turn the baby, like with a foal?"

"We can try. Get me some water. Clean water from a canteen."

Thaddeus Strickland hurried to comply. Holten talked soothingly to the girl and leaned forward to smooth her hair. He described the difficulty once more and insisted that she allow them to help. She might die otherwise, he emphasized. She and the child. When the lieutenant returned, Holten washed and reached out to the stalled baby.

Gently he eased the child backward toward its mother's womb. She wailed and thrashed her arms as the scout attempted to turn the infant in the narrow confines of her birth canal. With a gentle, continuous pressure, the tiny bit of life began to rotate. A small, wrinkled shoulder appeared. Then ever so slowly, a dark, fuzz-covered knob.

"Easy, easy," Holten chanted to himself. His patient screeched in response and gave a mighty heave of her mountainous abdomen.

The baby popped out.

"Like a cork from a champagne bottle," Lieutenant Strickland exhalted.

"He's here," Holten said tenderly.

A transformation had overcome the scout. His face

softened, eyes shining with pride and admiration. He lifted the squirming, squawling infant and exposed him to his mother's view.

"Uh—you've got to do something with the cord," Strickland said.

"Yeah. Tie it in two places and cut it free." Eli quickly did this and rocked back on his heels, using a spare neckerchief to wipe the baby clean. "It's—it's a real baby boy. And—I brought it into the world." He sighed out wonderingly, in a weak voice.

"Trooper Whitter, Trooper Thorne, please rise to hear the verdict," General Corrington intoned. When the defendants came to their feet, he went on. "It is the considered decision of this tribunal that you, Trooper Toby Whitter, and you, Trooper Neal Thorne, are guilty as charged. Having been tried and judged guilty by this tribunal, it is now the duty of the court to impose sentence, which we shall do forthwith. Trooper Whitter, Trooper Thorne, it is the decision of this court that you shall both be fined an amount of one half of your pay and allowances for a period not to exceed six months. Further, that you are to suffer corporal punishment in the form of a strappado, by manner of being latched to a wagon wheel, for a period not to exceed twelve hours. Such punishment to be executed immediately."

"No!" Toby Whitter shouted. "You can't do that to us! It ain't right."

"Oh, but we can," the general replied. "Believe me, Trooper Whitter, if we were still empowered to do so, we would have recommended a flogging. I have not finished with the sentence. You are then to be confined in the stockade for a period of one week, or until fit to return to duty. That is all. This court is dismissed."

"You don't understand," Whitter pleaded. "You can't do it. I—I'm too pale. I'll be burnt up by the sun. Please, don't do that to me. Anything, but not that."

"Then arrangements will be made to put you in the shade," General Corrington told the unfortunate trooper.

A detail of burly noncoms entered the court and went to where the convicted troopers stood. They grabbed the penitents none too gently and started to hustle them from the room. Toby Whitter began to sob wretchedly. The commanding general shook his head sadly.

Out on the parade ground, two giant wagon wheels had been erected to one side. The punishment detail brought the prisoners there.

Without a word, they quickly removed Thorne's shirt and long john top and hoisted him into position where his wrists could be bound to the top span of iron tire. Then his legs spread wide apart and some eight inches off the ground. His back stretched tightly over the hub. He groaned and began to mentally steel himself for the ordeal. His partner in crime, Whitter, hadn't the stuff of endurance.

Toby Whitter howled and writhed in the iron grip of his tormentors. He begged and offered all sorts of rewards to be let go. Beyond reason or logic, he alternated between promises of riches and blubbering self-pity. As his shirt came away, he nearly exposed Barryman's thievery ring.

"I've got money. Lots of it, fellahs. I got it hid away. I

can get more. Easy. I'll give it all to you. Only—please—please don't crucify me like this. I don't want to die!"

"Shut your mouth and take your punishment like a man," Neal Thorne snarled through his pain. He knew he had to quiet Whitter before the younger boy said too much.

Whitter sobbed and moaned as each wrist and ankle got trussed to the wagon wheel. When the men assigned the task had completed their work and walked away, he hung there groaning and mumbling softly for help. Slowly, the hours wore on. Six that day, six more the next. A wave of sickness rushed up from Whitter's stomach and he vomited over his own bare, hairless chest.

Late that evening, two dozen soldiers gathered out behind the sutler's store. They had been well lubricated on beer and cheap whiskey, and most were in a surly mood. Hot weather and boredom played a lot in this condition. When the last man arrived, Howard Barryman gave a nod to Vince Liscomb and stepped out in front of the group. Barryman raised his hands for silence.

"Men! I asked you here tonight to listen to something important that Vince Liscomb has to say. I know some of you are as angered by what happened to Whitter and Thorne as we are."

"Right."

"Y'er damn' straight on that."

"Quiet down, then. Like I said, we're a bit more than hot under the collar about this. Toby an' Neal are friends. Would you like to see any of your friends up there? Or yourselves? Oh, I know this has been done before and sometimes even justly. But we ain't in a war. There's no enemy outside the gates. What the hell's so big a deal about a feller slippin' a snort or two from a bottle of Panther Piss on a dull night? The officers have gone too far. Gen. Fat Ass Frank Corrington has overstepped his bounds. It's time something was done about it. But Vince can say it all better than me. Come out here, Vince and tell 'em what this is about."

"Thank you, Howard," Vince said as he exchanged places with Barryman. "Some of you men may not know it, but what the general did is against regulations. He's supposed to send accused parties on to headquarters for court-martial. And six hours is maximum that can be given for any offense punishable by being wheel-spread." What Vince neglected to add was that any general officer could convene a court-martial, and the regulations provided for six hours a day, for a total of twenty-four hours, or four days. By giving only half of that, General Corrington had been quite lenient.

"This sort of inhuman treatment can happen to you all. The officers have made themselves a law unto themselves. Long enough we have suffered under the oppression of an arrogant and tyrannical officer class. Long enough we have been subjected to showing respect and addressing these *bourgeois* pretenders as persons better than ourselves. But—it isn't true. We are ten times better than they are.

"They produce nothing. They consume more and better goods and provender than that allowed to us. They contribute nothing to society as a whole. They are classic examples of the hated petit bourgeois. Their continued existence stands in the way of the rising tide of the future! The time has come that we must stand up and resist opression. No longer can we endure the indignities visited upon us by these decadent figureheads of a discredited and bankrupt system. Two of our comrades are martyred out there on those wagon wheels. Who will be next tomorrow? Now is the time when we must rise up and wrest justice from the hands of the unjust. We must crush those who would hold us back, deny us our basic human rights. Soldiers of Fort Rawlins, unite! You have nothing to lose but your chains!"

A stout, though repressed cheer rose from the listeners. Deep rumble of angry male voices. It somehow reminded Barryman of his impression of the hungry beasts waiting to be let into the arena with the Christians.

"What can we do?" a trooper in the headquarters staff inquired.

"Nothing now," Liscomb responded. "The time is not yet right. Wait, watch, and be ready. You will be told."

After the highly successful meeting ended, Barryman and Liscomb remained outside, sipping beer "liberated" from the sutler's supply room.

"You almost had me believing that horse crap," Barryman told the compelling orator.

"You don't? It's true, you know. Everything I said."

"Oh, come on. You don't believe that four-bit word mishmash about the oppressed proletariat and the rising tide of social reform, do you? That's just more politician's bullshit to spread on our heads. Though it does sound like a promising way for a crook to get ahead. Rouse the stupid and the lazy and get them to do your killing and looting for you. Then step in and take over. It has class."

"You are a heretic and an unbeliever." Liscomb sounded personally offended.

"No. Only a realist. If this socialism stuff of yours can get these dolts to capture the fort, tie up all the officers and noncoms, then we can strip this place of everything salable. What's more, we can kill that bastard Corrington and all the officers, and *they'll* get the blame. Yeah, a full-scale mutiny is just the thing to make us that big score."

Myron Henshaw sat under the shade of an isolated blackjack pine and peered off into the distance. By his calculations he and his men could not be more than two day's ride from their goal. His most trusted follower, Blane Hollaman, squatted in front of him. Beside Hollaman stood Rufe Jenkins.

"Rufe. I want you to ride on ahead. We'll set up camp here for a while. Go northeast until you come to the fort. My man there may not remember you, but you'll recognize him right off. Let him know we're here. Tell him the wagons should be on the way right now. Then come back here and report what he has to say."

"Sure, boss. I'll head out right now."

After Rufe departed, Myron and Blane leaned back against the rough bark of the blackjack. Henshaw took small sips from a whiskey flask, washed down by large swallows of the water in his canteen. He raised himself partially and hollered over at the remainder of his eleven man group.

"Some of you boys get out and around. See if you

can't scare us up an antelope or something for supper. We'll need plenty of fresh game. Looks like we'll be here a while."

Eager to be moving, to do anything, four of the outlaw crew went quickly to their horses. Henshaw turned back to his second in command.

"Won't be long now an' we'll be all set to head south with our stock in trade."

"How do you figure we're going to get enough guns and ammunition to satisfy Cap'n Madonna and his free-booters?"

"That's up to our man on the inside," Myron told Blane. "We sent him to get in the army long enough ago that he should have some inside lines on what to do. From the letters he's been sendin' he thinks he can see to it we take everything that isn't nailed down. Once he gets the weapons and all the rest into our hands, we have it easy. Down to California and over into Baja, Mexico."

"Do you really think Cap'n Madonna is going to be able to pull this off? After all, Baja California is a big place. It's also a part of Mexico. They aren't going to take too kindly to having that much of their country liberated by a bunch of gringos."

"Might be so, Blane. But if he follows my advice, he'll take the southern end first. There's lots of gold, silver, and other valuable minerals to haul out of the mines in that area. It's desert and there's few people living there. Two hundred determined men could hold out long enough to leave there richer than anyone could ever dream possible. All I know is that I want to be a part of that. A big part, if you know what I'm gettin' at."

Myron Henshaw and Blane Hollaman exchanged knowing, secret smiles.

Shortly before dark, Lieutenant Strickland's command caught up with Gray Beaver's band. Riding in the van came Eli Holten and young *Peti-źan-źan,* with her new baby held proudly by the scout. Brightens-the-Lodge had explained to Holten and the lieutenant that she had not expected any trouble in delivering her baby. Although this was her first child, and despite her young age, she had not anticipated the need of a midwife or any female assistants for the childbirth. Her recent dilemma helped her calm her worries and accept the fait accompli of having had a man, and a white man at that, bring her son forth. That he spoke *Lakota* and called himself Tall Bear aided her in tolerating this breach of form. Still scandalized by a man, two men in fact, being present during this forbidden time, even more taboo than a woman's monthly bout with *iśnati,* she had begged they would tell no one. Further, *Peti-źan-źan* insisted, they must come with her to her husband and receive a reward for helping.

How she could reconcile the two, Eli Holten could not understand. When he rode into the camp, the *eyanpaha* heralding their arrival, he got another shock. Brightens-the-Lodge led him directly to the newly erected tipi of Gray Beaver. Smiling brightly, the lithe girl, seemingly little the worse for her ordeal, swung one leg over her pony and dropped lightly to the ground. She rushed forward and embraced Gray Beaver.

"Mihigna, I have brought you another brave son," she

declared.

"My heart is glad." A beautiful smile spread on Gray Beaver's face, and he lost his stern glower of disapproval. "How is it, though, that Tall Bear brings you here and that he holds our son?"

"I had foolishly chosen a spot of seclusion near to where the pony-soldiers halted their horses when they came to our trail. There were some complications with the baby. He hurt me mightily being born. I cried out—" *Peti-żan-żan* lowered her eyes, evading her husband's direct gaze. "Tall Bear came—after the struggle was over, of course, and helped me with the baby. If he had not, surely one or both of us would have died. I had been badly torn and needed to care for myself. Tall Bear washed the child and wrapped him in rabbit skins. He held our son and sang to him while I slipped away for modesty's sake and fixed my injuries. Then, after I had been fed and given a strong drink to kill pain, Tall Bear brought me here so that you might see your strong, handsome boy."

"I am grateful," Gray Beaver told the scout. He extended his arm and they clasped in friendship. "My lodge is forever yours if you wish to visit. If you ever have need, my pony herd and all I possess is yours to take from. Ask anything and it is yours. For truly, to have lost either of these most precious beings would have rended my heart."

Encouraged by this typical display of Sioux generosity, Eli decided to press his advantage. "I would ask Gray Beaver to return to the homeland of his famous band. The *Wipatapi* have always dwelled along the banks of Earth-lodge Creek. Now, with a new son to show the ways of his people, you must want strongly to do so in familiar surroundings."

Gray Beaver made a wry face. "That is so. There we find many quill. There is where we belong. I would see it again before the cold face of winter comes over the land. If it is as you wish it, I shall order the lodges struck tomorrow, and we will turn our faces toward the Snow Wind and return to Earth-lodge Creek."

"I am content."

"Then stay. It is time for a feast. We will roast dog and do a rack of hump ribs for honor of my newest son. You will sit in the place of respect to my left and fill yourself until you stretch your belly round like a buffalo cow paunch."

Smiling, with an affectionate arm around Gray Beaver's shoulder, Eli Holten readily agreed. Even the dog stew somehow sounded good.

Chapter 5

Myron Henshaw fretted through four dull, uneventful days. Occasionally he would join in the perennial poker game, or ride out with Bart Tanner, Buell Waller, and others to hunt for game to fill their pot. The weather remained hot, dry, monotonous. Only at night did a cool, stray breeze waft over their campsite. Henshaw thought he preferred ducking Apaches, or night-trailing to escape some posse to this enforced idleness. When at last Rufe Jenkins returned, the leader of this collection of border ruffians felt genuine relief. His messenger came directly to where Henshaw sat, carving fanciful shapes in the bark of the blackjack pine.

"Well? What did he say?"

"He's workin' on it," the taciturn Jenkins responded.

"What does that mean? Do we have a chance at a lot of equipment or not?"

"Suppose so. Said he wanted to talk with you direct,

before he put his plans in action."

"Another damned delay. What's this plan of his?"

"Dunno. He didn't say. I'll tell you one thing. There's a lot of unhappy so'jers at that fort."

"Oh?"

"Grumblin' 'mongst themselves, sneakin' around the lockup. Surly looks to anyone with rank or a stranger."

"Interesting. Think it has something to do with our man's plan?"

"Could be."

Part of his mind already lost in speculation, Henshaw smiled his thanks and added a jest. "You sure talk a leg off a feller, Rufe."

"Say what's needed."

"With the help of a crowbar, you do. Get yourself something to eat and a couple of drinks. I'll have to think about this meeting."

"Ain't as far as you think."

"What isn't?"

"Got to Fort Rawlins b'fore dark the day after I left here."

"Good. That much the easier for us. The wagons can wait here until we get word to bring them in. I'll head out tomorrow morning to meet with our man."

Gray Beaver's feast to celebrate the birth of his new son turned into a two day ordeal. Three buffalo, whose numbers grew scarcer each year, had been killed from a small herd grazing a few miles from camp. That necessitated a second, bigger banquet on the night following. This time, to the surprise of Lieutenant Strickland, the entire patrol was invited to participate.

It took most of the next day for the soldiers and their hosts to recover. At last Gray Beaver sent the camp crier through the circles of lodges with the familiar cry, *"Tikahpa! Tikahpa!"*

Quickly the tipis came down, to be folded, placed on travois and jostled into line for the march. This time the *Wipatapi* band turned their faces northeast, toward their homeland. Satisfied, Lieutenant Strickland watched them go. It took most of one day for the long caravan to clear the former site, so that their lodges remained in sight when the order came to make camp for the night.

By mid-morning the next day, the Quill Workers band of the Oglala had disappeared over the horizon. Strickland gave Eli a smile of relief.

"That's accomplished. Now we look for more, right?"

"Those are our orders, Thad. It was a good idea to send five troopers and Corporal Dooley along with Gray Beaver. It might prevent panic on the part of settlers, and it surely will remind him that he's given his word to return to his home."

"I thought you handled that magnificently, Eli."

"Luck had it we came on a band with a couple of new initiates to the Sun Gazing. That's bigger medicine than all the dreams ever to come from the Wise Ones. So they listened to me. Maybe next time we won't be so fortunate."

Following the lieutenant's earlier suggestion, the column of soldiers continued southward, while their course angled increasingly to the west. Eli scouted ahead, a good two hours beyond the point of the men sent out by Thad Strickland. Frequently he caught sign of varying-sized bands on the move. Gradually, they became fresher. On the third day beyond the meeting with the Quill Workers, the troops stopped for their noon rest and a light meal. One of the pickets Strickland put out along the back trail galloped into the circle of men as they washed away the remnants of hardtack and cold beans with scalding cups of strong, black coffee.

"Galloper coming in, sir!" he called out as his mount ground to a clod-throwing standstill.

"Ours?"

"Reckon so, sir."

"How far out?"

"Another ten minutes or so, sir."

The news, when it arrived, did not please Strickland in the least. He took the folded, wax-sealed dispatches from the courier and opened them one at a time. The first proved to be an unnecessary summary of the present situation, as seen by headquarters. The second, a bit more enlightening, since it had been based on reports of the messengers returning to Fort Rawlins from the three regiments in the field, came from General Corrington. It varied greatly from the official estimate of the situation.

"Other tribes, significant among them, the Crow and Arikara—traditional enemies of the Sioux and Cheyenne—have taken to this aimless wandering also," the general wrote in part. "It is reported by the Ninth Regiment that one might speculate that some occurrence has deprived the Indians of their natural homing instinct. They seem to have no direct goal, no purpose in their travels, beyond the spreading of some mysterious portent which had been revealed to them at the Sun Dance. Only two incidents of hostile action have been reported to this headquarters. Both ended amicably, without losses to either side. In most instances, the meandrous activities of the Indians encountered by our troops have been terminated and the subject bands set upon course for their usual winter habitats. Although there appears ample indication that some sort of curtailment of the Sun Dance ritual is necessary to prevent similar aberations in the future, it is the studied opinion of this officer that such a policy would only incur greater enforcement difficulties. Deprived of any religious outlet for their frustrations — for that is what the tribes of the plains surely consider the Sun Dance to be — hostility might be directed toward white settlers on the prairie, with the end result of involvement by the army. If some form of supervision or containment for such religious and social gatherings can be devised, it would prove to be far more efficacious."

Good, Strickland thought as he took note of the entry at the bottom, below the general's signature. "Copy to headquarters." Better still, he reasoned, if this totally sensible suggestion had been forwarded to the War Department and the Bureau of Indian Affairs. It had been the recommendation of headquarters that the Sun Dance be declared illegal and steps taken to prevent future participation. And how would they like a tidy little Indian war? Pondering the irony of it all, Strickland opened the final missive.

"Sergeant Reinhardt!" he called as his eyes took in the contents. A deep frown creased Strickland's forehead, and the corners of his mouth pulled down.

"Yes, sir?" the slender, patrician-nosed, very Teutonic NCO cracked out as he stopped before where Strickland sat, legs spread wide, a litter of paper around his feet. The yellow diamond inset in the downward-pointing three chevrons declared to the world that here stood the first sergeant of B Troop.

"Some not too pleasant orders from General Corrington."

"Jawohl, Herr Leutnant."

Despite his concern over the new assignment, Strickland had to smile. "Mention of higher command always effects you that way, Reinhardt. This isn't the Prussian Army, remember?"

"Jawo—ah, yes, sir." Reinhardt shrugged expressively, as only a German can. "It is only that I spent too long in the Junker Corps."

Strickland raised an eyebrow. "Oh? You've never mentioned that before. Your record shows only, 'Service in the Prussian Army.' "

"I was, for my sins, the son of a Junker and thus I served as an officer."

"By your adherence to spit and polish, I'd guess at least a captain."

"Major, sir. At least until my older brother inherited the family title and I decided to come to America."

"My God, an aristocrat in my company."

"Please, lieutenant, do not make—how you say—the tease."

Lieutenant Strickland produced a warm, friendly smile. "I didn't intend to needle you, sergeant. I'm sorry if I did."

"It is a sore place for me, sir. Here I want to be only what I am, Wolfgang Reinhardt. Had I been born first, I would be Wolfgang Albert Johann Maria von Klepfer, *Graff von Klepfer und Reinhardt.*" Reinhardt raised his hands in a helpless gesture, palms up. "But I was not, so I simplified my name and joined your army. Soldiering, you see, is the only trade I know."

"You'll be doing a bit more of it," Strickland informed him, raising the set of orders in his right hand and shaking them lightly. "More in line with your former service, too. Orders from General Corrington."

"Yes, sir. And what are we to do, sir?"

"I am to detach five men, an NCO and myself, along with Mr. Holten and locate a late-running wagon train of pilgrims headed to Washington Territory. Under your command, the remaining troops are to be taken northwest to rejoin the regiment. Lockhart and the Pawnee, Broken Tail, will continue to scout for you. The orders are effective upon receipt, so we will split up after the noon break and go our separate ways. Good luck, Wolf."

Despite his Prussian rigidity, Reinhardt grinned. "Thank you, sir. And the same to you. But, if I may speak, sir? A wagon train? This late in summer and no further than here?"

"That's correct. We're to see they return to Fort Rawlins until this situation with the wandering tribes is reconciled. That will probably close off further travel for them this summer. For which good deed we will receive no thanks from the civilians."

"*Ach!* Civilians. What do they know?"

"I'll keep that in mind, Wolf. I think I'll take Corporal Boyle with me."

"A good man. That will leave me three troop sergeants and four corporals. Enough, I think."

"See to it, then, will you, first sergeant?"

"Yes, sir."

When Eli returned, Strickland broke the news to him. The scout frowned, shook his head in exasperation and summed up the cavalry officer's speculations in a few words.

"That can mean a lot of trouble for us."

"We'll be making camp soon, Miss Hettie," the wagon train captain said in a deep, rumbling voice that nearly purred.

"I'm quite aware of that, *Captain* Reamer," Hettie Dillon replied coldly. Her snapping black eyes crackled with the distaste she felt from the wagon boss's attentions.

"I thought, ah, that after supper, ah, we might take a little, er, stroll?" His ruddy complexion, capped by a bulbous, crimson, "whiskey" nose, glowed in his eagerness.

That insufferable man! Hettie Dillon bristled as though he had made a graphically indecent proposal. "I think not, *Captain* Reamer. I am much too fatigued for such diversions."

"Sorry to hear that. But, a little postprandial promenade, down by the creek, or out under the stars might be just the medicine you require."

A wheel on Hettie's wagon squeaked insistently, adding yet another irritant to her tightly stretched patience. Dust rose, and the oxen of the wagon behind hers in the column took it to mind to low mournfully in protest to their labors. It hardly improved her outlook.

"Isn't that against your regulations?" she chided frostily, with a toss of her rich, dark brown curls. Brow puckered in concentration, she quoted verbatim from the list of dos and don'ts circulated to everyone who had signed on to Yellowstone Frank Reamer's latest yearly train west.

" 'No one to go outside the wagon circle after dark. No one to leave the inner compound at any time except in company with at least two others.' Am I getting it right?"

Reamer's close-set, pale blue eyes glittered with anger at being taunted so and he ground his yellowed, horsey teeth before he made answer. "Word for word, Miss Hettie. Only them rules is for the pilgrims. They don't apply to me an' the boys."

His grammar was as atrocious as his manners, Hettie considered. "Oh? Then are the *boys* going to accompany us?"

Reamer uttered a short bark of laughter from deep in his barrel chest. "Not likely. I'd have their scalps on my warshirt for sure if they tried it. The way I figgered it, you probably would appreciate a little privacy with me in them circumstances."

Reamer's brazen look took in her trim waist, small, firmly upthrust breasts, and the creamy complexion of her heart-shaped face. A sensual leer curled his thick lips as he gazed at her with a boldness that bordered on insulting.

Hettie widened her eyes, her face assuming a mask of sweet innocence. "Me? That I'd wish to be alone with *you*? Whatever would cause me to desire so unsuitable a thing as that?"

The jibe scored deeply, Hettie felt pleased to note. Frank Reamer's little, icy eyes grew a few degrees paler and colder as they opened in an astonished start. The fleshy lips thinned as he formed a knife-slash of disapproving mouth. For a moment she thought he might lash out at her, strike her with that ridiculously pompous, fake-Indian riding crop he always carried. Then the seething in his roundly protruding chest subsided. Crafty meanness crept into his close-lying orbs and they glittered malevolently.

"Missy, a spinster schoolmarm, well gone over her twentieth year, ain't got room to turn down an offer like mine. Why, you're well past yer prime. Won't be long before the gray starts movin' into that purty hair of yours. Where you gonna find a man willin' to crawl twixt your legs then?"

Crimson rushed to Hettie's face. Her mouth gaped, and she fought to force out words sufficiently scathingly to take this lecherous brute to task. How dare he! When she found her voice, she could only splutter. Reamer fueled her anger by laughing at her.

Braying lustily, he tipped his hat and leaned in closer to her so he could speak in a seductive whisper. "I'll see ya after supper, Missy. Then you an' me can go have us some good times."

Chapter 6

"You mean to say that you're going to lead a *mutiny*?" Myron Henshaw gulped out after hearing the plan of his agent planted in Fort Rawlins.

He stared across the table in the Thunder Saloon in shocked disbelief at the nondescript figure of Howard Barryman. The two of them had been in Eagle Pass only long enough to have exchanged greetings and for Barryman to disclose his plan on how to obtain the maximum amount of military supplies for Henshaw's project. Knowing Barryman's background, Henshaw would never have expected such a proposition from the slightly built, dirty blond-haired young man.

Barryman had fled to the frontier to escape arrest and prosecution for the murder of the attractive young wife of a former business associate. He had not committed his senseless act in a fit of passion, nor in a brutal and destructive manner. Coldly and calmly, because she had refused his advances, he contrived to get her alone. Then he shot her in the ear with a derringer. The choice of such a diminutive weapon, a two-shot, .41 rimfire "ladies gun," seemed to fit when Henshaw learned of it.

Howard Barryman had a soft, cloying voice, almost effeminate. Which matched his boyish features and curly, brownish yellow hair. He had the misfortune to have a roundish head that only emphasized the protrusion of cup-handle ears that contributed to an overall appearance of effete decadence. In a word, Barryman looked the perfect fop.

Hardly the type Henshaw would expect to be leading a mob of muscle-bound, sweaty, hairy-eared soldiers against their superiors in a mutiny. He had supposed he might hear a plot about mass poisoning, or similar "clean-handed" solutions to the problem in question. As Barryman spoke, Henshaw winced at the tone.

"Well, actually, I have gotten marvelous help from an unwashed social agitator named Vincent Liscomb. He has an incredibly mesmerizing voice and a way with words that could charm birds off their perches. Listening to him I got the idea. I had already run a test project to see how much and how often we could remove things from the fort without arousing a lot of attention."

"And?"

"It would take entirely too long for your purposes. Utterly impossible." Had the men at Fort Rawlins heard him speaking, none would believe that this was the same Howard Barryman they knew. Why, they would declare, this feller sounds downright sissy.

"So you came up with the idea of a mutiny. What settled you on that, may I ask?"

"Two of the dolts I recruited to help me steal salable items from the quartermaster stores got drunk on duty and were court-martialed. It all went rather fast, with three regiments in the field right now. They're in the stockade now, recovering from being strung up on wagon wheels. Due to be out tomorrow. It didn't set so well with a lot of the enlisted men. Vince began to whip them up over it and—" Barryman smiled nastily. "Whenever you say the word, I think we can deliver you a full-scale mutiny, complete with open gates for your freight wagons and a long delay to aid your getaway.

"Of course," Barryman said, continuing on a different tack, "after all this, I'll be a doomed man in the army. About the best I could look forward to is hanging. So, when you leave here, I expect to go along. It is my desire to be a very rich man. I want in on the action in Baja California."

Henshaw's eyes narrowed. "You know about that, do you?"

"Oh, yes. Not everything, naturally. Only bits and pieces you've let slip. Some free-booter named, ah, Madden—er, Madon, something like that."

"Madonna. Captain Madonna. He and his men have sold their services to several countries to help them fight their wars. Now he has this big design for the peninsula of Baja California. Take it from Mexico and turn it into a huge free state. A haven for guys on the owl hoot. There's also seaports for anyone who wants to try a hand at piracy. Lots of willing women, and he intends to get more. They make wine there and beer. Madonna thinks he can set up a distillery to make the Mexican national drink tequila."

"A regular little paradise." Barryman smirked. "What does he expect the Mexicans to be doing all that time?"

"You know that and I know that, only—Well, I think perhaps that our friend, Captain Madonna, has been around the Horn a few too many times. There's still unbelievable wealth to be wrested out of the peninsula, though. So, all right. From here on out, you're included in on the Baja gamble. If you pull this mutiny off, what can I expect in the way of supplies?"

"There are six cannons on the post. Two twelve pounders and four six pound gallopers. Lots of ammunition for them. About seventy-five rifles and an equal number of Springfield carbines. More than ten thousand rounds of ammunition for those. Blankets, a field surgical kit, uniforms, a rack of some thirty new Colt revolvers, the forty-five caliber models, some sabres, boots, tack and saddles, field glasses, and two artillery telescopes. Those have the range adjustment grids in the front lens. Cook pots, pack saddles, all sorts of other loose stuff. Not to mention the liquor and beer at the sutler's store. He's also got flour, sugar, coffee, beans, a lot of staples. Same for the army food supplies."

"I—I never imagined something so extensive. I've someone else working in this area. From that person's reports, I got the impression Fort Rawlins was a rather primitive frontier outpost."

"Three regiments stationed there. Which gives us an enormous amount of goods to select from. Why hasn't your other agent contacted me?"

"I considered it prudent for you to operate independently. For the safety of the mission, you understand.

Each has his own task to perform. Now, to the point, the freight wagons will be within a short distance of Fort Rawlins within three days. When do you propose to have your mutiny?"

Barryman laid a steady gaze on Myron's eyes. "It has to be before the regiments come back. Would four nights from now suit?"

"Excellent. I wish you a lot of luck, Howard. Now that we're to be partners in the Baja expedition, everything you can round up for us is on the bonus side. Only—get me the contents of that fort."

White canvas tops, stained now by weather, stood out against the prairie grass like arrogant, overlarge mushrooms. Eli Holten stopped on the brow of a hill and looked down on the middle branch of the Immigrant Route. The shoddy appearance of the train drawn up for night camp below him rubbed his sensibilities raw. Great gaps appeared between wagons, a sloppy practice not to be tolerated in hostile country. The livestock had been picketed outside the circle to graze. What an inviting target for some wandering Sioux. He saw little evidence of weapons ready at hand. It wasn't his train, Eli decided with a shrug, and they would have an army escort from now on. He turned away and rode back a different route than the one he had taken.

Lieutenant Strickland's cavalry detail reached the bedded down wagons two hours later. A dark scowl covered the florid face of the man who stepped out to greet them. He held up a hand, signaling that the soldiers halt a good thirty yards from the circled train.

"What you so'jer boys doin' snoopin' around here?" Reamer demanded as he swaggered up to where Holten and Strickland sat their mounts. The odor of whiskey fumes rose with his breath.

"Who are you?"

"Reamer's my name. I'm cap'n of this train. I'll ask again, in case you be hard of hearin'. What are you so'jer boys doin' snoopin' around my business?"

"Mr. Reamer, we've been sent here by—"

"Yellowstone Frank Reamer?" the scout interrupted to ask in a frigid voice, tinged with distaste. Holten had heard a lot about Reamer—all of it bad.

"I be, if it's any business of yours."

"I'm making it so."

"Sorta smart-mouthed for a civilian scout. Who might you be?"

"Eli Holten."

Reamer had been glaring at a spot somewhere near the center of Sonny's broad chest. At the sound of the scout's words, his shaggy head snapped up and his ruddy complexion lost a bit of its whiskey-induced hue.

"T-the one they call, Tall Bear?"

"That's what my Sioux friends call me," Eli answered.

A petulant curl came to Frank Reamer's lower lip, which he protruded as he digested this information. "You've crossed horns with some friends o' mine, Holten. That's something a man don't readily forget — or forgive."

"It sounds like that's your problem, not mine." Eli rested his hand on the shiny grip of his Remington revolver.

"I can make it your problem," Reamer challenged.

"Gentlemen!" Thad Strickland snapped. He had never seen his friend Eli on such a prod before. "We've come here on a matter of army business, Mr. Reamer. There are large bands of Indians on the move west of here, some hostile, some not."

"Hell, that's true anytime," Reamer replied.

"Not in these numbers. Our best estimates now are a figure of slightly over ten thousand braves. Add in the usual number of women and children and it makes an impressive count. They are spread from here in Dakota Territory, through Montana and Wyoming. My instructions are to escort your train back to Fort Rawlins until the situation can be resolved."

"You can forget that, brass-buttons. Why, if we don't push on now, we won't make the passes before winter sets in. So turn around and take yer yellow-striped horse nurses back where they came from. A handful of Injuns ain't gonna trouble Yellowstone Frank Reamer none."

"You seemed to have missed my point," Strickland persisted diplomatically. "Listen closely. There are *ten thousand* or more warriors out there, along with women and children. Their whole pony herds. And they're all filled up with some mystic dream they say has to be carried to all the tribes."

Reamer snorted derisively. "Lot of plain nonsense. I've never seen ten thousand fuckin' hostiles in my life and I probably never will. What kind of greenhorn do you take me for? You can't get that many Injuns to ride together, let alone fight side by side. What's more, with their squaws an' brats along, they prob'ly wouldn't fight nohow." Reamer made a show of calculating on his fingers, as though totaling the number of Indians.

"Why, that'd take in damned near the whole of the Sioux Nation, the Cheyenne, and a half dozen other tribes."

"It does," Holten injected. "He's telling you the truth, Reamer. Are you too stupid to recognize it? The Sioux and their cousins, the Cheyenne, gathered for a big Sun Dance. They are still out, away from their home territories and off the reservations. They are singing songs about wiping out all the white men and defeating the army in one big, spirit-directed battle. The thing is, the other tribes are listenin' to them. Even their enemies, the Crow and the Arikara. They haven't done anything yet, but for your purposes, you might as well consider every one of them as hostiles."

"Shit. You'll have to come up with something more than that to convince me."

"How about an Oglala arrow through that empty head of yours?"

"Why, you son of a—"

"That's enough!" Strickland thundered. "Mr. Holten, would you be good enough to scout back along the wagon trail and join us in the morning before the departure. I will remain with my detail and do what I can to convince Mr. Reamer of the wisdom of this course of action." He turned to the irate wagon boss. "It's not that the army is trying to be arbitrary. There is good reason to believe that the sight of a caravan of whites would push some of the more hotheaded too far. I mean those who came in from the Yellowstone country and remain, technically, hostiles. Surely we can sit down together and talk this over. Let me explain more thoroughly what odds you would be facing out there all alone."

"I got my reputation to think of. Nope. There's no sense in talkin'."

"What reputation?" the scout snapped. Then he turned to Lieutenant Strickland. "It's no use, Thad. I told you he was too stupid."

"You're askin' for a killin', you skunk bastard," Reamer said growling at the scout.

"That will do, Mr. Holten. Please be so good as to follow my instructions."

"Yes, lieutenant. As you say, lieutenant." Holten reined Sonny around and set spurs to the stallion's flanks.

As the big Morgan jumped forward, the scout felt a sour taste of self-disgust. He had acted childishly. Both his friend, Thad Strickland and that incompetent asshole wagon guide, Reamer, knew it. He'd tried to shame a man with a reputation for incompetence and cowardice into agreeing. It had failed.

"Well, you know, lieutenant," Eli heard Reamer begin. "I think about this a bit an' maybe you're right. Let's go fill up on some coffee, and chaw on it a spell. I got me a bit of the ol' Who Popped John to give that Arbuckles a zing, if y'er a mind for it."

The words lifted Eli's spirits. You never knew. His ploy might have worked after all.

"Bring yer boys in, too." Reamer was going on out of earshot of the scout. "It's about time for grub. We've some mighty fine cooks on this train. Nothin' like a meal, whomped up by a female to warm a man's heart."

As the embers of the cookfires pulsed in dying glory, Lt. Thaddeus Strickland accepted a cup of strong coffee from Frank Reamer. Stoutly laced with raw whiskey, it sent a double fire down his throat. Corporal

Boyle and his men had gathered around, as had the five crew members working for Reamer. Strickland examined these latter with growing unease.

One, a scout who looked as though he couldn't find his way to the outhouse on a sunny day, had an·odd cast to one eye. Milky colored, it seemed to have a mind of its own and looked off at odd angles in a disconcerting manner. Another, a short, rotund Mexican who wore a derby hat, herded the spare saddle stock and draft animals. He seemed to be afflicted with a permanent erection, a protuberant fact that was, after a short·while, impossible to avoid noticing.

Reamer also had two hunters along, to provide fresh meat for the paying customers as well as the captain's table. A pair of rangy, pig-dirty individuals, obviously brothers, they had shifty eyes and scraggly teeth, that went well with their carrion breath and filthy clothes. Lastly came Reamer's cook.

Slope-shouldered, bowed as though by the troubles of a wearysome world, the grizzled oldtimer seemed to use a vocabulary consisting of every obscene and blasphemous word in the English language — and nothing more. His steady stream of profanity shocked and scancalized the ladies accompanying the wagons to Washington Territory. In truth, his blue-tinged blasts embarrassed Thad Strickland somewhat more than he at first realized. As the conversation progressed, they edged closer, taking up a semicircle position behind Boyle's troopers.

"So you can see the army's position, Mr. Reamer. We are here to protect you. Right now all three regiments from Fort Rawlins are in the field, attempting to stop this senseless migration of the Indians. As a result, it is impossible for us to provide you an escort. It's only sensible, then, for you to turn back to the fort."

"An' what happens to our schedule? How long's this roundup gonna take? Ya see," he went on without giving time for a reply, "you have no idea. Am I right? Well, then. We'd be stuck here in those howlin' blue northers all damned winter if we did what you said."

"Not necessarily."

"I say we would. That ain't gonna happen, my fair young lieutenant. No sir. We pull out in the mornin', headin' west accordin' to plan. Ain't that right, boys?"

Five hammers ratcheted back, and the cavalrymen found themselves looking into the dreadful muzzles of a quintet of .45s.

"Yeah, boss," the nearly toothless cooked drawled. "It's howsomever you say."

Chapter 7

"First one of you who whitens a finger on his trigger dies." The granite-hard voice of Eli Holten came out of the dark.

The tableau of unsuspecting soldiers and their captors held for only a second longer. Then the scrape of steel against leather filled the tense silence as Lieutenant Strickland drew his service revolver and eared back the hammer. The big .45 muzzle centered on Frank Reamer's chest. Then Eli stepped into the lighted circle by the fire.

"I heard you went in for some shady practices, Reamer," the scout told him. "But I didn't think it included drawing down on the army."

"Corporal, relieve these men of their sidearms and any other weapons you find," Thad Strickland commanded.

"Gladly, sir," Corporal Boyle responded in a cheery note.

"Now, see here," Reamer began to protest. Grinning, Strickland poked him in the chest with his Colt. It silenced further complaint.

When the assortment of knives, revolvers, and knuckle-dusters had been gathered, the officer holstered his weapon. Holten did the same. Then he stepped in close to Frank Reamer and gave him a solid, roundhouse right to the side of the head.

Frank Reamer went down in a blur of arms and legs. Growling with anger, he sprang upward nearly as fast. His first punch caught Eli in the stomach.

Air whooshed out of the scout's mouth as he blocked a looping left and stepped in on his opponent. Eli's short, punishing right-left-right combination sent Reamer stumbling backward. He slammed into a water barrel and nearly lost his balance.

Reamer recovered in time to block a whistling right that would have seriously mangled his left ear and weaved away long enough to set up his own attack. It came in a windmilling fury of fists. Blood flecked his knuckles as he found a vulnerable target on Eli's face.

The scout absorbed the punishment and retaliated with a solid kick to Frank Reamer's groin. The blow missed, though it caused considerable pain to Frank's right thigh. The wagon boss nearly went to his knees, staggered away and stooped to grab a handful of loose dirt. This he hurled at the scout's eyes as he rushed at Eli again.

Instantly, three of Reamer's crew edged forward, reaching to pin the scout's arms.

"Hold it!" Strickland barked at Reamer's cohorts. The Colt appeared in his right fist again.

"You're a dead man, Holten," Frank snarled as he

advanced once more, a three-foot length of trace chain in one hand.

Wise in the ways of brawlers, the scout said nothing, saving his breath for the contest. His face stung from three shallow cuts, and his ribs had absorbed enough punishment to make him favor his left side slightly. He backed away from the menace of the whirring links and darted his glance around the area for some form of nonlethal defense.

He didn't want to kill the trail guide, merely whip him into submission. There would be difficulty enough escorting the wagons back to the fort. It would only be compounded by not having the services of the wagon master and his crew.

"Ya want I be shootin' this spalpeen bastard?" Corporal Boyle drawled in a heavy Londonderry accent.

"Leave him, Jim," Eli answered back. His gaze settled on a broken ax handle, cast aside by the immigrant who had been using it. He faked a dodge in the opposite direction, then ran for the oak shaft.

Reamer anticipated him, and the trace chain whistled through the air, a scant inch from the scout's face. Eli tried a kick, while his enemy remained off balance. It missed but caused Reamer to retreat and attempt to whip the chain around again. Holten's hand closed on the smooth haft of the ax handle.

He spun toward Reamer and snapped out with a prodding blow that thumped solidly into the paunchy middle of the wagon boss. Reamer bellowed and backed off. With careful deliberation he began to swing the chain in a windmill pattern in front of him. Holten prodded him some more, while the soldiers shouted encouragement and Reamer's men supported their boss. Eli saw an opening and went for it.

Bright splinters of pain radiated from the scout's right forearm as the steel links smashed down on it. Wincing to hold back a cry of agony, Holten jerked his arm away before the sinuous metal links could wrap around and trap him. Swiftly he switched hands and made a feint toward Reamer's eyes.

Instinctively, the wagon master jumped backward to avoid being blinded. He made a bad mistake.

For an instant the chain went slack. With a two-hand grip, Eli swung the ax handle. It smashed solidly into Reamer's rib cage.

"Unnngh!" Immobilized by overwhelming waves of torment, radiating from two shattered ribs, Reamer dropped the chain.

By that time the scout had reversed the direction of his blow and brought the oak staff up in an overhead position. With a grunt of effort Eli sent it swishing through the air to crack loudly against the top of his antagonist's skull.

Reamer's eyes rolled up and he sagged to the ground. A soft sigh fluttered his lips as he struck the hard-packed soil.

"Now I'll scout the trail," Holten panted as he faced Strickland. Only slowly did he become aware of the large gathering, which included nearly everyone on the wagon train. He shook his head in an attempt to clear it and spoke to them.

"This train leaves in the morning for Fort Rawlins, like the lieutenant said. Anyone with further objections can take them up with me or Corporal Boyle."

"Sure an' I'd be lovin' a good donnybrook about now," the corporal informed his audience.

Holten turned away and started to walk to where he had left Sonny. Suddenly he sagged and had to grab at the side of one wagon to support himself.

"You're hurt!" he heard a musically sweet feminine voice cry out. Then a gray haze, through which he perceived his surroundings only vaguely, descended over him.

Myron Henshaw sat at the fireside in the temporary camp set up by his men. With him were Blane Hollaman, Bart Tanner, Lenny Spears, and five more of his murderous companions. Henshaw had a look of confidence and anticipation on his face.

"Barryman is set up in a real sweetheart of a deal. He's going to seize that fort, and then we're going to empty it like a rat-infested whorehouse."

"How the hell's he gonna do that?" Hollaman demanded, dubious of such an ambitious enterprise. "There's too damned many soldiers in a place the size of Rawlins."

"They're all out in the field, chasin' down stray Indians," Henshaw explained. "Can't be more than fifty men at the fort. Most of them are behind Barryman's mutiny. The way he explained it, all they have to do is seize the officers and the noncoms and the fort is theirs. He's going to break out all of the booze at the sutler's and keep the ones not in on our deal drunk while we scoop up everything in sight. By the time they sober up, or enough troops to do something about it get back, we'll be long gone."

"Hey, that shines," Bart Tanner enthused.

"We'll be halfway to Baja California before the army

figures out what really happened," Henshaw went on. "Of course, there is the telegraph. We'll not be able to take any of the well-traveled trails once the word goes out. There'll be soldiers from here to hell and back looking for us."

"How do we stay out of their way?" Rufe Jenkins asked.

"By bein' where they ain't," Lenny replied.

"That's close to what I had in mind," Henshaw told him. "They won't know *exactly* where we're going. It will be a good week before the search is extended wider than Dakota Territory and surrounding states. There's a lot of land between Fort Rawlins and Mexico. We'll head due south until we cut the Santa Fe Trail, then take it as far as the middle of the Cimarron Cutoff, then south again across the desert. There's not that many troops in New Mexico Territory. Nor in Arizona as we well know. Once we're a good distance to the south of where the major search will probably be conducted, we head west to California, then down into Baja."

"What about the Apaches?"

"Fuck the Apaches!" Henshaw declared emphatically. "According to Barryman, we'll have seven or eight artillery pieces with us. How long can those thick-headed animals stand up against that?"

"Yeah, boss, I *do* like your style," Lenny chortled.

Soft, warm fingers pressed gently on Eli Holten's right forearm. "You're lucky he didn't break your arm," Hettie Dillon remarked with concern. "Our Mr. Reamer is a beast who walks on two legs."

"You don't sound too pleased with him," the scout answered through a faint smile.

"Oh, that man!" Hettie blurted in exasperation. "I could go on for days—one for each we've been on the trail from St. Jo. He-he's a lecher, a braggard, and a bungling incompetent. Granted, I am not expert in the field, but I do know when something is being terribly mismanaged. This wagon train is a prime example."

Holten hadn't heard much in that sort of vocabulary for a long time. Back before he ran away to the frontier as a matter of fact. It made him think of Miss Troast. So reasoning, he put his reflections in words.

"You talk like a school teacher."

"I am," Hettie told him. "I'm on my way to Seattle to take a position in their new school. Think of it!" she enthused. "They have a single school that employs seven teachers. Why, that compares with some of the best in the East."

"You'll have your work cut out for you, I'm afraid," Eli told her.

"Oh? You've been there?"

"No. But it's nearly as unsettled there as on the frontier."

"Hummm. I'll not bandage this arm," she decided. "Those cuts on your face need attention, though."

When he had stumbled against the wagon and this attractive young woman came forward to aid him, Eli had not been at his best. More observant now, he felt a strong attraction to her. Not so much for her offer of succor, but for a raw, lusty physical appeal she evoked in him. She couldn't be much over twenty-three or four, he decided. Her long lashes, bottomless black eyes, small mouth, and dark brown hair gave her a pert, gamine appearance that belied her maturity. He felt a familiar stirring and leaned closer so she could dab at his cut cheek with a damp cloth.

"You've been more than kind in your attentions to me, ma'am."

"Call me Hettie and the pleasure is all mine, Mr. Holten. What is your given name, by the way?"

"Eli. Ow!"

"I told you that would smart a bit," Hettie replied as she continued to daub horse liniment onto the split skin. "Give that a day or two and I'll trim off that little flap with my embroidery scissor. Would you like something to drink, Eli? For the pain, I mean."

"Yes. That would be nice."

"All I have is some elderberry wine."

"My God! Elderberry wine. I haven't had any of that since I started sneaking it out of my mother's cabinet when I was twelve."

Hettie smiled, a gesture of pure radiance to the scout. "Well, then, we'll have to correct that deficiency right now." She rose with flowing grace and climbed the small set of steps to the rear of her wagon.

When she returned, she carried a dusty bottle and two crystal goblets which, her delay suggested, had been necessary for her to dig out of storage. She brought with the items another of her bright smiles.

"I've been saving this for a, ah, special occasion, Eli. The downfall of Captain Reamer seems a fitting time." She poured and handed a glass to the scout. Then her words took on a more serious note.

"Frank Reamer might be all that I said, but he is also dangerous. I sometimes believe he is capable of any violent or dishonorable act. Please be careful

90

around him, Eli."

"Oh, I will, you can count on that, Hettie."

Hettie smiled and placed her fingertips lightly on Eli's cheek. "I'm glad. I wouldn't want anything to — harm you." She shook her head and sent those gentle fingers to the scrapes and cuts on Eli's face. "Now isn't that a foolish remark. These — these are hardly love bites."

Her casual comment surprised the scout. Such language from a spinster school teacher? He examined her guileless face for some clue and found, to his pleasure, an intensely ardent reflection of his own sensual awareness.

"I would that they were. Then they might not smart so much."

"Oh! I'm sorry, Eli. Did I make it worse, touching them?"

"Not at all, Hettie. I'd be willing to swear that you have the healing touch."

"Oh, pshaw now, Eli." She actually blushed, Eli saw with bemusement.

"I mean it, Hettie. I feel much better. And the wine is delicious."

"It's from the last batch my late father put up. He died five years ago, so it's had time to come to full maturity."

"Yes. It has a ripe richness about it — like the lovely and gracious lady who served it."

His gaze held hers a moment and she became, as current fashion described it, flustered. "W-would you like more? It doesn't keep well, once the bottle is opened."

"Thank you. It allows me to share your company a

bit longer."

Though she reflected a downcast gaze, her voice held a warmth and richness as Hettie replied. "You don't need any excuses to share my company, Eli."

They talked quietly while the stars wheeled half-way through their nightly course. The elderberry wine bottle got emptied and Hettie produced another. Despite his growing interest in this lovely woman, Eli found his head nodding. The long day, the fight with Reamer, and the late hour combined to rob him of energy. They sat close together and expressing concern over his injuries Hettie frequently touched him lightly, though not always on his wounds. At last he could keep sleep away no longer and rose to leave.

"My goodness. Here I've kept you up half the night and a big day ahead of you tomorrow. I don't know what's come over me." She stood, also, and inclined herself slightly toward him.

Eli reached out with his good left arm and encircled her trim waist. He drew her near and kissed her lightly on the lips. At least it started out lightly.

A torrent of passion exploded from her soul and warmed their buss into a fevered joining that promised much, much more. He felt her lips part and probed with his tongue, against small, even white teeth, that opened to receive his exploration. When they broke their long embrace, Holten noticed that his pulse pounded and his heart raced within the confines of a chest gone tight. He cleared his throat roughly.

"What do I owe you for your medical services, Hettie?"

"N-nothing. You've more — ah, more than amply paid me now. Sleep well and I will see you in the morning, Eli."

"More likely at night camp. I *do* have to scout the trail a bit."

Chapter 8

A soft breeze moved the tall strands of buffalo grass in imitation of the undulating bosom of a mighty ocean. Meadowlarks trilled their cheery calls, and an occasional rustle indicated the rapid departure of a rabbit. The thin, high clouds had begun to form into denser puffballs of white as the sun slanted down the sky toward nighttime. Despite several minor break-downs, the wagon train, nominally led by Frank Reamer, had managed to cover a distance that Eli Holten estimated to be some thirteen miles. For a first day, it seemed promising. The caravan halted early.

Gleaners, under the protection of two troopers, went out to gather windfall wood from a stunted but stub-born stand of pine that commanded a knob of a hill some two hundred yards north of the trail. Women constructed hasty fire rings from rocks gouged from the creek bank by their menfolk, and soon small blazes began to crackle. Throughout the day, Reamer and his crew had performed their duties with surly reluctance. Holten and Lieutenant Strickland discussed the matter and considered them sufficiently subdued to pose no threat. Accordingly, Eli relaxed and rested his sore body.

By the time the fires had burned down and nearly everyone in camp had eased into well-deserved slumber, Eli sought the company of Hettie Dillon. Her effulgent smile instantly raised his spirits. She rose on tiptoe, eyes closed, and he dutifully kissed her lightly.

"You look tired," she commented.

"I am, Hettie. I don't know why it is, but each year it seems to take longer for the hurts to go away."

Hettie nodded sympathetically. "You can't reverse the course of nature. No one grows younger, you know."

"You're a philosopher, as well as master of primer and grammar books?"

A musical peal of laughter came from Hettie Dillon. "Would you like some more wine?"

"You should be saving that," Eli protested. "If it is all you have."

"I can't think of anyone I would enjoy sharing it with more. But—" She brightened and reached inside the chuck box on the side of her wagon. "I did locate something you might prefer."

Hettie produced a bottle of Loch Morahn whiskey and proudly displayed it. "I swapped some sugar and a piece of bacon to Mrs. McBirney for it. Whiskey from Scotland." She poured two fingers in a pair of glasses, added water to hers, and handed the other to the scout.

Eli drank deeply, smacked his lips in appreciation, and enjoyed the subtle explosion in his stomach. It had a similar effect to Frank Corrington's fine brandy, only with a slight smoky taste.

"Mrs. McBirney called it a 'single malt,' whatever that means."

"It's delicious. Sort of—warms a man."

Hettie's gaze held level with his and smoldered with not-too-hidden a meaning. "It has the same effect on a woman."

"Hettie, let's take a little stroll away from these fires. I want you to see the prairie sky like you've never had opportunity before. It—dazzles a person."

A small hand to her mouth stifled an impish giggle. "You're waxing poetic, Eli."

"Why, thank you, Hettie."

Arm in arm, they walked off into the now dormant tall grass.

"We've had a dry year," Eli commented in a low voice. "Not enough rain. Usually this buffalo grass is taller than a man's head."

"How do you see the stars then?" Hettie teased.

"All you have to do is look up."

Hettie did as instructed. A vast dome of blackness, richly sprinkled with more stars than she had ever known existed, appeared to expand before her eyes. As she continued to stare into this unfathomable depth, it seemed to rotate slowly. Then faster, until she lost her equilibrium and reeled drunkenly into Eli.

"Oh, Eli," she gasped. "A person could get seriously lost looking up like that."

"Actually, the stars help guide us," Eli responded in a fit of prosaic directness. All the same, his arms went around Hettie's shoulders and drew her close for an ardent kiss.

Hettie's knees buckled, and Eli eased her weight and

his down among the sheltering, concealing slips of buffalo grass. His fingers found the buttons at the back of her dress and began to undo them. Hettie moaned softly and ran one small hand down the flat expanse of his chest. Then she, too, began to work on the fastenings of his shirt.

"Oh, yes, Eli. Hurry. I—I dreamed of this all last night, like a nervous schoolgirl."

"You filled a lot of my night, too," the scout told her sincerely.

A crisp rustle accompanied the removal of Hettie's dress. She sighed as Eli cupped one small, pert breast and began to manipulate her nipple through the thin cloth of her chemise. Her hand dropped lightly to the front of his buckskin trousers and began to gently squeeze the rigid swell of his aroused manhood. Deftly she freed the lacings and fasteners and liberated that long, fat shaft to the cool night air. Her fingers closed around it and began to stroke with the assurance of ample experience. Eli continued to part layers of feminine clothing and revealed her dainty, alluring charms.

After an appreciative moonlit examination of her largess, Holten bent forward and took her right nipple in his eager lips. He worked it until the nubbin of flesh responded, growing rigid with her burning desire. Then he nipped it playfully with his strong, white teeth. Hettie moaned in delight and increased her pressure and speed.

A shiver of sublime pleasure rippled over the exposed surface of the scout's skin as Hettie's nimble fingers played an amorous tune on his throbbing instrument. He broke off his earlier ministrations to spread her knit shawl and ease the trembling young lovely into position on her back. Slowly he rose above her, and Hettie stared fascinated at his swaying pole. Her pale, creamy flesh shimmered before him, and he took a long, enjoyable look at it, absorbing into memory each delightful curve, protrusion, and the inviting promise of pink-tipped breasts and sparsely furred mound. Languorously, Hettie spread her legs.

Never slow to respond, the scout sought her innermost secrets with probing fingers, relishing the steady flow of warm moisture that signaled her readiness. Hettie cooed with delight and wriggled under him, one arm extended, so that her fingers could make fleeting, tantalizing contact with the ruby tip of that masterful phallus that swung so impudently before her eyes. At last, Eli began to lower himself between her legs.

"Eli—this—this isn't my first experience. Even so, be tender. It's been a long, long time."

With patience and absorbing skill, Eli brought his maleness into the wispy threads of silken pubic hair and explored the outer lips of her fevered portal. Images of serene pastures and stately bowers filtered through the scout's consciousness as he brought more pressure to bear and felt the parting of the rosy petals at the gates to Hettie's paradise. With carefully managed restraint, he eased his way inside the lush garden of rapture.

As he did, Hettie shivered through his entire length and hastened to impale herself on more of Eli's bounteous endowment. With each passing second of the gradual insertion, waves of happiness washed over them both. Nothing, their pounding hearts told them, could compare with the magic of their union.

Dawn came to Fort Rawlins with calamitous results.

Corporal Lancing, the trumpeter, roused groggily, dressed and started to the parade ground with his shiny brass instrument tucked securely under his left arm. He met a knot of grimly silent men, several not in uniform, under the porch overhang of the barracks. Before he could even inquire what brought them from their sacks so early, they seized him and thrust a dirty sock in his mouth.

"Tie him up and be quick about it," Howard Barryman ordered in a whisper. "We've got to take care of the guards next."

"The ones on their posts or in the guardhouse?" Neal Thorne asked in a hiss.

"Take the walls first, dummy," Howard snapped. "There's more of 'em to face in the guardhouse, and we don't want men with loaded rifles at our backs."

"Yeah, sure, sure," Thorne muttered, wounded by Barryman's sharp reply.

Quickly, the seven mutineers spread out and headed individually for the sentry posts. Stanley Greene, in his position atop the main gate, saw them and grinned. He alone among the men on guard that night would not be knocked unconscious. A member of the mutiny planning committee from its first known meeting, he looked forward to tormenting some of the officers and NCOs who had made his life in the army a continuous hell.

Not inclined to be industrious, Stanley had always sought ways to avoid work as a boy. Or he would contrive to do the absolute least he could get away with. He carried this deleterious habit into adult life.

Quick to blame others for his own failings, he made an ideal conspirator.

Greene's part in the plot was simple. He had to make sure the big gates did not swing open until ordered so by Howard Barryman. No one opposed to the mutiny was to be allowed to escape. In the case of officers, they were to be captured. Noncoms and enlisted men seeking to get out would be shot. Stanley relished this latter order. He had scores to settle with at least three sergeants. Greene licked thick lips in anticipation and wiped at the scratchy patches of a sparse, blond beard that smudged his jawline. How he hoped one or more of them would try to break out the front gate! From a distance he heard the plan go into action.

"Halt who goes there?" came a challenge from the stable area.

"It's me, Ortega, Barryman. I'm stuck with shit shoveling detail and thought I would get started early."

"All right, Barryman. Come ahead."

A meaty smack and soft groan sounded a moment later. Greene glanced off to his left and saw another mutineer approach the guard at the door to headquarters. The soldier came to port arms and issued his challenge. Stanley's muddy brown eyes widened when he saw a knife in Butler Bell's left hand, held out of sight along the seam of his trouser leg.

"Hey, Granger, cut the snap-shit routine. I gotta see the sergeant major before reveille formation," the conspirator remarked in an offhand manner.

That brought him closer to his victim. The knife flashed in the air a moment before it dug deep into Granger's stomach. Bell ripped upward and spilled the hapless sentry's intestines on the porch. Massive shock, brought on by overwhelming pain, prevented the dying trooper from shouting the alarm. Stanley Greene felt sick and fought off a wave of nausea as Bell gave a wicked cackle and started out in search of another target.

"Oh, God. Oh, holy shit," Greene gasped out.

This wasn't anything like Vince Liscomb and Howard Barryman had said it would be. The mutineers ran to complete their assignments now. Only a few minutes remained before the next changing of the guard. A piercing scream came from the doorway of the armory. Someone had messed up their kill.

"Corporal of the guard! Post Number Seven," a trooper yelled from the wall. "Trouble on Post Five!" A second later, he shrieked and pitched over the parapet, a slim-bladed knife thrown by Vince Liscomb stuck in the left side of his chest.

Instantly the door to the guardhouse flew open. Framed in the lamplight from behind, Corporal Allen paused long enough to catch a bullet in his forehead as the first shot of the mutiny exploded across the parade ground.

Yelling men seemed to appear from everywhere, converging on the guardhouse. Several carried firearms, and Stanley Greene had no idea which one might have fired the fatal shot. He trembled now, in the grips of terror. Most of the troopers assigned to sentry duty did nothing to resist. Angry shouts came from inside and two sharp reports as weapons discharged. Then Vince Liscomb and Howard Barryman came outside with Sergeant Tucker and Lieutenant Abel.

"Soldiers unite!" Liscomb shouted. "Crush the oppressors!"

Over at the armory, willing hands reached for Springfield carbines as Toby Whitter and Butler Bell handed them out.

"Hooray for the revolution!" Liscomb shouted. "Who'll join us?"

The armed men formed up under Barryman's direction and stormed along officers' row. More, as they obtained their arms, followed Liscomb along to the NCO barracks. The soldiers cheered lustily now, and the sick, sinking feeling began to recede in Stanley Greene's stomach. Caught up in the excitement he all but jittered as he watched from the platform above the main gate.

In only a few minutes, a handful of prisoners began to stream onto the parade ground. Officers in long johns, two entirely naked, several sergeants, who snarled at their captors. Among them, Greene spotted half a dozen privates. Before long, what appeared to him to be the entire portion of the garrison not involved in the overthrow had been assembled. While Barryman dispatched others to conduct a second search, a dark form detached itself from the side of the headquarters building and started toward the gate.

As it grew closer, the figure resolved into a man in yellow-striped cavalry trousers and an unbuttoned officer's tunic. Stanley hesitated a moment, then brought his Springfield to his shoulder. Despite the racket as the troopers ran amuck, the ratcheting of the heavy hammer sounded loud to his ears.

"Hold it right there, or I'll gun you down," Stanley declared in a quiet voice.

"I know you, Greene. You'll hang for this, if you join those others."

"Lieutenant Pierce!" His platoon leader.

Stanley Greene's bowels turned to water under the hard, demanding gaze of the young, brown-haired officer. "Uh — I — I'm sorry, lieutenant. I have to — er — no!" In a welter of conflicting emotions, Stanley Greene weakened and changed his mind. "Uh — hurry. Get out while you can. I w-won't say anything."

"I'll remember you for this, Trooper Greene. I'll do what I can to help your case," the courageous officer replied. Quickly he ran to the judas gate in the big double portals and disappeared out onto the prairie.

"Where's the general?"

"Where'd he go?"

Voices called in confusion from the parade ground. Men ran about shouting and slapping each other on the back. With a minimum of disturbance, the mutiny had gone off successfully. Only, Stanley gathered, more officers were unaccounted for than Lieutenant Pierce.

"The fuckin' adjutant's missing too," Butler Bell yelled from the head of officers' row.

"Try the headquarters," Stanley called to them, to atone for his lapse and direct attention away from the gate. "I saw some movement around there."

"Thanks, Stanley." Howard Barryman hailed him sarcastically. "You're a good boy."

Humiliation burned on Stanley's cheeks. Barryman had always given him a hard time, talked down to him and tried to pick a fight. Greene had joined the mutiny only because he thought it might buy him some relief from the petty harassment. It hadn't done him much good, he speculated miserably while he watched a dozen men surround the headquarters building while another six dashed inside.

Muffled shots crackled from the interior of the office complex. Curses followed, then more weapons blasted away. After a moment, while smoke boiled out through the open door, a lull came.

"You in there!" Howard Barryman's voice rang over the parade. "General Corrington."

"Who are you and what do you want?" the general's voice came faintly.

"You'll know who I am soon enough. Put down your guns and come out of there. We have your fort. Your officers and noncoms have been rounded up and are under guard. Surrender or die."

"You can go to hell, you son of a bitch!" A blast from a .45 Colt emphasized the general's profanity.

A fusillade erupted. Stanley Greene counted some fifteen rounds before Barryman shouted for a cease-fire. For an aching minute, silence held. Every man on the post strained to determine the outcome.

"You still alive in there, general?"

"I am. And so's Major Styles. You men out there listen to me. Mutiny is a hanging offense. Lay down your arms now and return to your barracks. If you do, I will personally see that you receive only perfunctory sentences in the stockade or a federal prison."

A chorus of catcalls and hisses rose from the embittered men of the mutiny force. "Tell us another funny one, general," one conspirator hooted. More boos followed.

"If you continue," Frank Corrington went on, ignoring the interruption, "you will suffer the full penalty of army regulations under the Articles of War. I'll personally tie the knots. Give it up, men. Return to your normal duties until this can be resolved."

"Go fuck yourself!" a soldier shouted through his laughter.

"You're going to die, you *bourgeois* oppressor of the masses," Vince Liscomb bellowed.

Several of the rebellious soldiers laughed.

"I'm giving you fair warning. You'll get the chance to tell your side of this, to have a proper defense, if you do what I say. If not—when the regiments return, you'll die fighting them or later on the gallows. You're all good troopers. Act like it!"

"You might as well be pissing up a rope, Frank," Major Styles told him angrily.

"We'll hold out. We've got to. I sent young Pierce to break free and locate Strickland's patrol. They can't be far away now, leading that wagon train back here. Even that should be enough men to put down this—this pencil-pusher mutiny."

"You'd better hope so, Frank."

"This is your last chance to come out, general," Howard Barryman announced. "If you continue to resist, we'll start killing your NCOs first. Then the officers. We won't make it easy on them. You've got one minute. The first one dies then."

"I think I recognize that one's voice," the adjutant told Frank Corrington. "A malicious little back-stabber and sneak named Barryman. He's one of the ones I suspect on the thievery."

"In the present circumstances, is that bad or good?"

"I'm not sure. To listen to him speak in his normal voice, you'd think he might fall apart from ennui at any second. There's a vicious streak in him, though. Be sure of that."

"Thirty seconds!"

As the early morning sun warmed the prairie, Yellowstone Frank Reamer rode his roan gelding up alongside a wagon driven by a pleasant-featured girl of fifteen. He tipped his hat and spoke softly to her.

"Good morning, Patty. I hope you're not, ah, put off at me like some of the others."

"Oh, no, Frankie," she gushed. Adoration shone in her clear blue eyes, and her heart speeded up at sight of the man she loved.

"That's good to hear. I don't know how I could bear it if I lost your affection," Reamer cynically informed her.

Frank Reamer had spotted the small-statured child the day the train formed up in St. Jo. From the wide-spreading way she stood and walked, he knew she had experienced a man, probably several men, before. In recent years, he had developed a passion for progressively younger, more sweet-faced girls. Patty Cramer fitted his needs well.

He soon observed that she eyed him with more than simple interest. Naked lust glowed in her eyes, and her infatuation made her bold in giving evidence of her desires. On the fourth night out, Reamer had led her outside the circle of wagons to a dark spot under a large willow. There he kissed her firmly and hotly on the mouth. In response, she reached down and grabbed his stiffening organ. In only seconds they had their clothes off and lay on the damp ground, grunting, writhing, and humping away in sweaty hunger.

After that, Reamer tapped her whenever he could. She could not get enough, hadn't been able to, she confessed to him, since her deflowering at the tender age of seven.

"It — sort of — grows on you," she had summed up in a voice of childish innocence. "It feels so good. What's wrong with it that people don't think the way we do?"

Now Frank had definite plans for horny little Patty.

"Oh, Frankie, can't we — well, you know. Do you think we — "

"Can see each other tonight?" Reamer finished, an expression of carnal desire coloring his face. "That's what I wanted to talk to you about. I'll be ready a while after everyone goes to sleep. I'll tell you where to meet me later."

Patty clapped her hands. "Oh, wonderful, Frankie. I love you, love you, love you."

Satisfied, Reamer rode away to take a place beside Lieutenant Strickland at the head of the column.

Chapter 9

"Ten seconds!"

Abner Styles looked anxiously at his superior. Frank Corrington shrugged, avoiding his adjutant's questioning gaze.

"There isn't anything else we can do," the general declared flatly. "All right. Hold your fire. We're coming out!"

Outside, on the parade ground, the regimental sergeant major of the Twelfth broke away from the cluster of closely guarded officers and noncoms. "No! Don't do it, general!"

A fraction of a second later, a single shot cracked. The big, tough NCO groaned and pitched forward into the dust, his left kneecap blown away.

"D-don't do it, please, sir!" he bellowed through his misery.

Another shot claimed his right knee.

"We're coming out, I said," the general repeated.

"No, General Corrington!"

Before the last word had left the RSM's mouth, another bullet smashed into his body, this time destroying a hip joint. Unable to endure the additional shattering agony, he screamed and writhed feebly. Howard Barryman stepped to the door of the headquarters.

"You really are a fool," he told the wounded noncom. Then he raised his revolver and shot the sergeant major neatly between the eyes.

Face livid with rage, painfully twisted in grief for a man he admired greatly, Gen. Frank Corrington stepped out beside Barryman. Two of the mutineers kept him under guard.

"You slimy bastard," the general thundered in a low, menacing voice. "If it is the last thing I do, I will see you swing on a long rope. No merciful neck breaking for a cowardly, goddamned assassin like you, Barryman. I want to watch your eyes bulge and your face turn purple. I'll applaud when your tongue pokes out of your ugly mouth and you bite through it while you make funny little noises as the hemp slowly strangles you to death."

"Save your pretty speeches for someone who appreciates them, fatass," Barryman snarled. His false bravado masked the beginnings of fear. He had seen the raging horror that lurked deep in Frank Corrington's eyes. It reminded him of the monsters who had haunted his dreams as a child. Like a small, frightened boy, he wanted to cringe away from what that look promised. He shook himself free of the icy grip of fear.

"Take all of the officers to the stockade, search and strip them of any weapons, then lock 'em up in separate cells."

"There ain't enough," one experienced trooper told him. "Not if you're gonna secure the noncoms, too."

"We'll put most of the rest in some solid building. Maybe the quartermaster warehouse. Double the officers up then, as need be. Get to moving."

Barryman stalked away, his mind busy on other matters. He had to send word to Myron Henshaw. The sooner those wagons came in, the better. First things first, though. He would have to get the liquor flowing from the sutler's store. Too many men who didn't know the whole story, had helped pull the mutiny off. Better to have them blind drunk and out of the way.

Less than a minute after the cell doors clanged shut on the officers and several NCOs of Fort Rawlins, General Corrington began to lay plans for an escape.

"We are going to get out of here," he declared to the others in a hushed voice. "When we do, we're going to string up these mutinous sons of bitches in carload lots."

All within hearing or sight of their commander listened with close interest. "The first thing is to overcome any sense of failure or desertion of duty at being captured like we were. There's nothing that could have been done to anticipate it or to prevent it from happening. Under the circumstances, it is better to be alive and able to effect an escape, than out there dead like the sergeant major. Now, with that out of the way, let's go on to what's next.

"It's my guess that these mutineers are going to get roaring drunk, whoop and holler for a while, then lay down to sleep it off. They'll wake up with tremendous hangovers and a lot of remorse. The smarter ones will desert. They'll get rid of their uniforms and try to lose themselves on the frontier."

"From the noise coming in our window, I'd say you're right, general," a gray-haired captain on the opposite side of the corridor declared. "There's a lot of window and bottle smashing going on, and I can see whiskey cases standin' on the porch of the sutler's store. What they did with him, I don't know."

"Probably shot him down," Major Styles offered.

"Only too true, Abner. Gentlemen, please, we have a lot of work to do. First off, I need an inventory of everything we managed to bring along into here. No matter how insignificant, tell Major Styles about it right away."

One by one the officers reported. A surprising amount of jailhouse contraband came to light. Nearly every officer had a box or two of sulpher matches. One young lieutenant, Clark Abel, who had the night duty as OOD when the mutiny began, had been hustled inside so quickly that his captors had failed to remove his holster and pistol belt. His revolver had been taken, but he had two cartridge pouches, each with a pair of loaded cylinders. That gave them twenty-four rounds of .45 ammunition. Three of the officers, including General Corrington, had pocket knives. Then came the usual collection of pencil stubs, paper, pocket change, and a couple of plugs of chewing tobacco.

"It's not a lot, but with it we have a start. Abner," General Corrington ordered, "I want you to organize a tunneling commitee. Not to dig a real tunnel, of course, but try to pry the mud mortar out of these walls. Somehow we must weaken the structure enough to force our way through."

Outside, an attentive, if slightly drunken audience listened while Vince Liscomb regaled them with stories of the capture of the fort. Many had not been in on the original attack on the guards. When he concluded, a towheaded private stood to ask a question.

"Now that we got them officers locked up, what are we going to do with them?"

Liscomb grinned wickedly. "We're going to hold us a trial, convict them of abuse and a lot of other things, then we're gonna execute the bastards."

"How? What's you got in mind?"

"You know, we're not the first successful proletarian revolution. The French had one in 1789 to 1798. They deposed the monarchy, took over control of the National Assembly and eventually brought the aristocrats to justice. It was a bloody revolution, made the more so by a man named Dr. Joseph-Ignace Guillotin. During the Reign of Terror, as the middle years were known, both the aristocracy and the hateful bourgeoisie where systematically exterminated.

"You see, Dr. Guillotin invented a humane device for execution of condemned prisoners. One that had the added advantage of being a machine and thus able to be used on both nobles and commoners alike. For days on end, the heads rolled into baskets, severed from blue bloods and rich commons, as it should be. They rode to their deaths in tumbrils, little horse-drawn carts, bound hand and foot. There in the Place d'Revolution, they were made to climb the blood-splattered steps to the platform of the doctor's marvelous device. The executioner had them jerked off their feet, placed on a long board, their heads through a yoke device that kept them pinned there while he yanked the lanyard, and the weighted blade came crashing down. Off went the head and the crowd roared.

"Several old women had rocking chairs at the edge of the clearing around the guillotine. They would sit, knitting, while the aristocrats were led to their doom. Often they would raise high the shawls they made, to be dyed by the rich, thick blood of the blade's victims. Oh, it made a real spectacular show. Such displays, after all, are the stuff of good revolutions."

"We gonna do something like that to our officers?" a dubious soldier inquired.

Vince gave him an ingenious stare. "You never know. We just might."

Frank Reamer waited in a small draw a safe thirty yards from the encampment of wagons. He paced the sandy bottom and cursed the Fates and Eli Holten for putting him in such a position. To be dependent on the moods and whims of a barely nubial girl stuck in his craw. They made the beast with two backs rather well together, but beyond that, and the fact she was a few bricks shy of a load, what did he really know about her? Could he rely on her to do what he wanted? The only sure thing was she loved to screw. She'd hump a snake if someone would hold it still for her. Mightn't a handsome army officer in his pretty blue uniform turn her head?

Or worse, he considered in mounting anger, the buckskin-clad figure of Eli Holten ought to make her flood her bloomers with desire. Where would he be then? A crackle of small branches alerted him to someone's approach. Automatically his hand went to the empty holster at his side.

"Shit!" The muffled curse escaped his lips as he ducked low.

Patty Cramer stepped through the screen of tall grass into the open bottom of the wash. Her face, in the dim light of moon and stars, radiated her eager anticipation. She rushed into his arms.

"Oh, Frankie, I—I could hardly stand it, waiting so long. See?" She took his hand and slid it up under her dress. She wore no underclothing. "I'm all wet and shaking just thinking about—us."

Frank kissed her, his tongue probing deeply into her willing mouth, while his fingers explored her slippery mound. Patty put both hands down the front of his trousers and began to squeeze and stroke his hardening organ.

"Oh, hurry, hurry. Put it in me," she begged.

Reamer nearly gagged. He steadied himself and forced the words out. "Sure, honey. Get your clothes off. First, though, there's something I want you to do for me."

"What's that, Frankie?" Patty inquired in a coy, little girl voice. "You want me to suck it like I did before?"

"That would be nice, but this is something important. You know they took my guns and those of my crew? If this is such dangerous country that we have to turn back, that leaves us helpless, doesn't it?"

His logic might be faulted by others more knowledgeable, but it made sense to the girl. She nodded, all big-eyed and flushed with lust. "Y-yes. I suppose so."

"Well, then, what I want you to do is find out where those guns are kept."

"Oh, I know that."

"Good girl. There's more. Since you know, I want you to wait until the soldiers quiet down tonight, then slip out and get our guns. Give them back to us. That way we can protect all of you if something happens."

"Won't the soldiers see them?"

"No. We'll keep our weapons hidden until trouble comes along."

"Ummm. Well, I think I can do that. If—if you love me real good tonight."

"Oh, I'll love you plenty good, all right. Better than ever before."

"Wonderful." Patty removed one hand from her eager activity and opened his fly.

Reamer's trousers sagged down around his knees as she knelt on the sand and opened her mouth. Warm and moist, the tender tissues closed over his raging manhood as shivers raced up his spine. She'd do it. Deep inside, as the talented little girl worked on his fiery shaft, he knew she'd do exactly as he said.

No food was brought to the stockade that evening. Hunger cramped the bellies of the confined officers and NCOs. Already Frank Corrington had two groups working diligently with knife blades to scrape loose the mud and grass mortar that held the thick blocks of sod in position to form the outer walls of the cell block. He sat in dark contemplation and tried to will young Lieutenant Pierce to succeed in finding Strickland's patrol and Eli Holten. The door to the guardroom slammed open, and three drunken mutineers swaggered into the corridor. In the lead came Howard Barryman.

"We-l-l, look there," he drawled in his soft voice, the fingers of one hand stroking the lobe of a cupped ear. "It's Sergeant Manahan. Got any more holes you want dug with a spoon, Manahan?"

"That I do," the NCO snapped. "Yer grave, ya fuckin' bastard."

"Oooh! He's a fiesty one, isn't he? We'll take the stuffing out of you soon enough in here," Barryman snarled.

Beside him, Vince Liscomb tugged at the black swatch of hair that hung over the left side of his forehead. "Do you think we should tell them now?"

"Why not? This seems like an appropriate time. You can make the announcement, Vince."

"Please, *Comrade* Vince, if you don't mind. Let's find the general."

Two cells further on, the insurrectionists came to where General Corrington sat on a narrow, wooden bunk. Major Styles recognized all three, and the general had no difficulty identifying Toby Whitter.

"Drunk on duty, now this. You've sunk to a new low, Whitter," the general declared.

"Hold your tongue, *bourgeois* scum!" Liscomb barked. "Listen closely. This decree is for all of you. The Soldiers' Revolutionary Committee has decided to grant each of you a fair trial. Your many crimes will be detailed before you, and then judgement will be passed. It would be advisable for you to make a full and voluntary confession of your many misdeeds and place yourselves on the mercy of the People's Court.

116

Self-criticism is the first step toward awareness, which leads to revolutionary solidarity. Acknowledge your crimes, be purged of them, and join us!"

"In a pig's ass!" a stocky captain shouted. The left side of his face was swollen and discolored from a blow he received during the takeover.

"Well, we'll see, won't we?" Liscomb sneered, uneffected by the outburst. "The trials begin in the morning."

Chapter 10

Goldenrod, blue and white thistle blooms, and wild buckwheat blossoms nodded in stately clusters of color in the slight, early morning breeze as Eli Holten saddled up and rode away from the wagon train to check the trail ahead. Already men jingled trace chain as they hitched their teams and made ready for the day's journey. The soldiers kept close watch on Yellowstone Frank Reamer and his men as they went about their duties. Holten paused below the brow of a gentle rise and looked back. A soft smile of contentment creased his leathery brown face.

He had spent another magnificent night in precipitously abandoned lovemaking with lovely Hettie Dillon. Dedicated to her profession, she had been giving the scout a liberal education in a variety of obscure and maddeningly erotic sex practices. He had become an apt pupil. He sighed contentedly and rode on, his mind reaching back to the hours before dawn.

"There, Eli. Let's try it this way," Hettie had urged. Her long fingernails traced over his lean, hard body, over every scar and muscle.

Hettie rose and placed herself in a net hammock she had strung between the trunks of two sturdy lodge pole pines. With one graceful gesture she beckoned the scout to her side. "Climb in," she said, wrapping one hand around the swollen evidence of his arousal.

Somewhat awkwardly, Eli followed instructions. The unfamiliar contrivance swayed precariously and, for a moment, Eli thought it might turn over and dump them both onto the ground. Hettie looped a leg over each of the canvas strips sewn to the edges of the swaying bed and squirmed herself into a better position. Still wary of an ignominious fall, Eli knelt between her thighs.

"I love it so much," Hettie sighed as she caressed Eli's flat abdomen and worked her way again to his rigid penis.

It swung before her, long, supple, and ready. She leaned forward and kissed the ruddy tip, teasing it with her tongue, then reclined once more and guided the pulsing spear to the top of her moist cleft. During the night they had made love three new ways, and now she trembled with excitement, anticipating her latest invention.

"Think of the fun all those sailors have," she whispered.

"There are no women on their ships."

Hettie wrinkled her nose. "Nevertheless, it ought to be exciting—for us." She had at last talked the scout into it. Now the amorous couple paused on the edge of the consummation of another adventure.

"Hurry, Eli. Fill me up and let's set this thing to rocking," Hettie said panting.

Slowly, Eli parted the outer lips of her treasure trove with a firm, steady pressure on his tingling maleness. He added greater force as he slid into position at the ferns that shaded her secret passage. Like a good gardener, he inserted his digging tool slowly, so as not to disturb the vibrant, living thing he sought to divide. Prepared at last, he thrust forward and felt the heavenly sinking sensation as he slid smoothly into the well-lubricated passage. Tender tissues surrounded his solid phallus and his heart swelled, the world seeming to swing to-and-fro.

"Eeeeiii!" Hettie wailed behind a muffling hand as his huge bounty cleaved a path to her inner chambers.

In counterpart to their own swaying motion, the hammock began to sway from side to side. It only served, as Hettie had predicted, to heighten the enormous pleasure they derived from the slightly naughty means of coupling. After that astounding fete of carnal transcendence, they had rested and talked of Hettie's plans for the future.

"I want to become a pioneer in the field of education," she had declared strongly. "There is so much that could be done. Classrooms need more and better facilities, so that children don't have to cramp their work onto tiny slates. It should be the responsibility of the school board to provide paper and pencils, other supplies and books. I dream of the day when every class will be in a room devoted to a single grade level. Surely the recitation of other students must be a deterrent to the others learning what they are supposed to be studying."

Although completely lost in this, to him, an esoteric subject, Eli listened and mulled over her statements in light of his own school experiences. Somehow, he felt her ideal classroom lacked something. To him it had helped to hear what the older pupils worked on. Prepared him, so to speak, for the years to come. He held his peace, though. After all, she was the professional, not he. Before long, their mutual need and desire overcame the philosophy of education, and they once again entered the Elysian fields of love. Remembering it eased the miles as the scout journeyed far to the east of the slow-moving wagons.

When Eli Holten had departed, he failed to notice the smug smiles on the faces of Frank Reamer and his men. "Now we're gonna take our wagon train back," Yellowstone Frank had promised his followers.

"Ya mean we're gonna up an' pull iron on the soldier boys again?" Drake Ferrel, the cook, inquired.

"Nope. We've got the means," Reamer said as he patted the revolver hidden under his shirt. "But we've got to have a better opportunity."

Shortly before the noon stop, Frank Reamer saw his chance coming right toward the train. Some two dozen Sioux, including women and children, approached warily, making the plains' sign for peace as they drew closer. Lieutenant Strickland rode out and talked with their leader. After a few brief sentences, he came back.

"They say they mean no harm," he announced to the anxious people of the wagon train. "They are riding everywhere to spread the word of the big medicine at the Sun Dance. Their leader did say they could use some sugar and coffee."

Reamer snorted derisively. "Is that all their chief could do? There's your big danger, brass-buttons. Beggin' for coffee like a whipped dog."

"He's not a chief, Mr. Reamer. It's just a large family party. Two brothers, a couple of cousins, their wives and children. I think we ought to give them the coffee and sugar. The army will reimburse you at Fort Rawlins."

"Like hell!" Reamer snarled. "All we gotta do is run them redsticks off. Shoo 'em right outta here. That'll stop their whinin' and beggin'."

"They are Hunkpapa Sioux," Strickland explained patiently. "Sitting Bull's people. It wouldn't be wise to antagonize them. They are peaceful enough now, but it shouldn't take much to rile them. The army will round them up soon enough and send them back to their homes."

"We'll make 'em peaceful, right enough," Reamer declared from the saddle of his roan. "Teach 'em some manners they won't long forget." He dug spurs in and jumped his mount toward the silently waiting Sioux.

Mounted likewise, with the exception of Drake Ferrel on the small crew wagon, Reamer's followers surged out behind him. At his direction, they all produced their weapons. At less then thirty yards, they opened fire on the Indians.

"Oh, shit, we're in for it now," Lieutenant Strickland gusted out. "Circle the wagons. Corporal, ready your men. Everyone with a rifle, or other firearm, prepare to repel attackers."

On the slope, some hundred yards from their families, the seven warriors looked on during the demonstrative discussion at the rolling-wood lodges. When some of the white men left and rode their way, they expected to receive the promised treats of the sweet and bitter powders.

Instead, they got sizzling lead.

Bullets cracked through the air around their heads, and one slug scraped hide from the neck of Skyfire's pony. The animal whinnied painfully and reared, then began to prance about. Made nervous by the noise and smell of blood—these were travel horses, not war ponies—the others began to nicker and flinch their loose hides. Broken Bow raised his lance into fighting position and saw his brother, Lazy Elk, do the same. The whites came closer.

Another fusillade broke the silence of the prairie. This time Crooked Nose yelled in a high, keening voice and fell from his pony, blood streaming from a large hole in his back where the slug had come out. What had gone wrong?

Broken Bow pondered this as he signaled his companions to turn about and ride back to their families. He and the pony-soldier had given the sign of peace. They talked in a friendly manner and agreed that to smoke and drink some of the bitter drink would be good. Then these men came to attack them. Would there be more?

Too many white men to fight in the open, Broken Bow decided.

Quickly the Sioux rode back to their women, children, and pony herd. "We must go beyond the hill," Broken Bow ordered. "We have to think on this. But first we must discourage the bad whites."

"Why has this been done, husband?" *Ikusanwin* asked Broken Bow.

"That is what we must decide. Go, quickly. Take the horses and the children beyond the ridge."

Along with the remaining braves and three older boys who joined them, Broken Bow turned back toward the charging whites led by Frank Reamer. He and his small force took careful aim and fired with arrow and musket ball. The projectiles found only two of the five men.

A big .65 caliber musket ball cut a deep, painful gouge along the outside of Issac Kilgore's right thigh. He howled in pain and rage and swung away from the determined resistance. Blood streamed down his leg. The charge faltered, and Frank Reamer glanced to his left to see a arrow protruding from Hank Leach's left shoulder.

"Give 'em one more round, boys, and let's hightail it," Reamer commanded.

"We just gonna leave em?" Pete Leach demanded indignantly. "Look what they done to my brother."

"We got 'em on the run. That's what we wanted," Reamer snapped at him.

Forty-fours cracked once again as the warriors retreated over the brow of the hill.

On the far side, angry voices argued at Broken Bow to take the battle to the whites. After all, they were the ones to break the oath. Broken Bow recalled how Crooked Nose had been killed without even a weapon in his hand.

"We will fight. You, *Kehala*," he told one of the excited boys, "ride to the west. Find our brothers, the Quill Workers, and tell them of this battle. Ask that they send men to help us against the many guns of the whites."

"I'll ride my swiftest pony, Broken Bow."

"Good boy. Stop for nothing until you find them."

The fourteen-year-old ran to his horse, clutching at a bag of jerked buffalo he wore at his waist, glad he had thought to put it on that morning. Behind him, Broken Bow spoke calmly to reassure his followers.

"Now we go see what is being done by the whites."

Yipping with victory, Frank Reamer led his men back toward the wagons. They had easily routed the cowardly Sioux, he gloated. Now that the guns were out in the open, they'd take care of the soldiers as easily. When they rode into the clearing formed by the circled wagons, Frank looked up into a ring of Springfields.

"Keep your hands clear of iron," Thad Strickland said ominously. "If you hadn't gone and stirred up so damned much trouble, I'd have my troops cut you all down where you stand. As it is, we might need every gun we've got. Get down and put your horses up. Then find a place around the circle. Do it all right carefully; there'll be a Springfield at each of your backs."

Liscomb's talk of the execution of aristocrats during the French Revolution had its desired effect. The malcontents and malingerers who had readily joined in the mutiny whipped up popular sentiment for a similar ghastly fate for the officers of Fort Rawlins. Contrary to the general's prediction, the morning's hangover did not produce any desertions of the fort.

Instead, hammers and saws lent their familiar sounds to the day's routine as construction of a guillotine began at the carpenter's shop. Sparks and black smoke belched from the stack as amateur blacksmiths put their hands to the forming of fittings and the huge, bloodthirsty blade. In the headquarters building, the court-martial room had been made ready and a tribunal selected from the members of the Revolutionary Committee. At eleven o'clock, Howard Barryman sent for two of the prisoners: General Corrington and Major Styles.

"You have been brought before a tribunal of the People's Court, as authorized by the Revolutionary Committee," Vince Liscomb intoned in the archetypical drone of a judge. "We will hear the list of your crimes and decide upon a verdict. Before you are pronounced guilty and sentenced to die, you have one final opportunity to save yourself.

"Throw yourselves on the mercy of the People's Court. Admit your guilt and ask for a suitable punishment. Rip those shameful symbols of aristocratic power from your epaulets and join the workers of the world. After a suitable penance for your past crimes, you will be allowed to share in the fruits of our new, classless society."

"At least we've been elevated from the *bourgeoisie* to the aristocracy," Frank Corrington said sarcastically.

"Silence!" Howard Barryman thundered from the center of the tribunal. "The People's advocate may proceed."

Swiftly, Butler Bell revealed a long string of imagined crimes and abuses, painting the commanding officer and his adjutant as only slightly less reprehensible than Simon Lagree. Half of them sounded like childish pique at a loving parent's mild discipline. The rest originated solely in the warped brain of Vincent

Liscomb. At the end of this parade of lunacy, a long silence ensued.

"Are we going to be permitted to refute this ludicrous list of immature whining?" General Corrington demanded.

"Only your advocate is permitted to speak," Howard Barryman replied softly.

"And who is that, may I ask? There is no one at the table with us."

Barryman permitted himself an ironic smile. "Why, who better than the most eloquent Comrade Vincent Liscomb?"

Corrington and Styles exchanged knowing, defeated glances. The general wanted to groan. He also wanted to wrap his fingers around Barryman's neck and squeeze until the fopish misfit's eyes popped out of their sockets.

"You can shove that right up your ass," Abner Styles growled.

"You refuse counsel? You waive your rights to rebuttal? Very well, then. It is the duty of this tribunal to reach a verdict and render judgement."

Barryman glanced to left and right, then back to the prisoners at the bar. "By unanimous vote of the tribunal, you are found guilty as charged."

"What a surprise," General Corrington snapped. It earned him a rifle butt in the back.

He let himself groan this time as he lurched forward. Butler Bell steadied him and directed the general back to his chair. Aching, a red mist of anger fogging his eyes, General Corrington eased himself downward and waited beside his friend.

"You will remain standing," Barryman demanded.

"And you saw to it that I cannot," the undefeated general returned.

"Never mind. The outcome will be the same. You, Gen. Frank Corrington, and you, Maj. Abner Styles, have been found guilty of heinous crimes against the people. It is the sentence of this tribunal that you shall be held in confinement until the twenty-sixth day of this month, at which time you will be given over for execution. The means prescribed for your death shall be by guillotine. This tribunal is adjourned."

"Mark me well, Barryman," General Corrington rumbled. "You'll burn in hell before you lop off this head."

"Not at all, my dear general. Not at all."

After the condemned prisoners had been returned to the stockade, Howard Barryman summoned Toby Whitter to his office, the one commandeered from the general. Barryman sipped Frank Corrington's fine brandy and puffed on one of his hand-rolled Havana cigars.

"Toby, I want you to ride to the southwest of here, along the old Columbine Trail, to a camp you'll find a day and a half from here. There will be some big freight wagons waiting. Tell a man named Myron Henshaw that everything has been done. Have him bring the wagons on in. By the time we chop off Corrington's head, I want this place stripped to the bare walls."

"Yes, sir. I'll leave right away."

Howard Barryman patted his small paunch and sipped more brandy as the young ex-soldier hurried from the room. Then he turned to where Vince Liscomb slouched in a large, overstuffed, leather-bound chair.

"You know, I'm a great deal smarter than Henshaw."

"I've, ah, noticed you held that opinion," Vince replied dryly.

"He may have set up this Baja California deal. But it is I and only I who can deliver the goods. Once I know the details, it should be an easy matter for us to seize the initiative."

"For what purpose?"

"Simple, Vince, ah, Comrade Vince. We can become absolute masters of Baja California. With your help and that of those who have proven loyal to the mutiny, we can go along with Henshaw only so long as it aids our plans. Then, when the time comes, we will seize power and reap the benefits of everything Henshaw plans to do down there. Brilliant, no?"

Chapter 11

Although well traveled, the branch of the northwest immigrant trail that went past Fort Rawlins had few homesteads along its westward length. Afoot, Lt. Tom Pierce alternated trotting and walking through the long day after his escape from the mutinous soldiers. He slept fitfully on the hard ground and started out two hours before daylight. By mid-morning of the second day, he managed to commandeer a saddle-broken mule from a lonely dirt farmer who stubbornly clung to the land despite droughts and fearsome winters.

Pierce started off at a gallop, only to soon discover that the mule had a mind of its own. After much cursing, rib kicking, and angry brays, the young officer had to settle for a bone-jarring, kidney-punishing pace only somewhat faster than a walk. All the same, it carried him steadily onward to his goal. In the end, he didn't find the wagon train. Eli Holten found him.

Birds twittered noisily around a small seep-pool of

muddy water, and giant-eared jackrabbits hopped lazily beyond the fringes, waiting a turn to slake their thirst. Eli had ridden toward the fort for five hours before stopping to mark his progress with a cairn of stones. On the way back he would set up similar signposts at likely camping spots approximately a day's wagon travel apart. Fortunately, he thought, that would be only two. Another day beyond this furthest indicator would put them within hailing distance of the fort. His task completed, Eli decided upon a smoke before starting back.

From a carefully wrapped package in his saddlebag, he took a slender, slightly crooked cigar. Its dark mahogany-hued wrapper had weathered well, with only a shred of leaf loose at the blunt end. Eli bit off the twist at the rear and spat it out. He touched a lucifer match to the ring of his cinch and it flared into sulphurous life. Gratefully he drew the smoke into his mouth, savored it and expelled half before he inhaled shallowly. A good-tasting cheroot, he acknowledged. He stiffened at the distant sound of thudding hoofs.

Damn! Just when he'd started to enjoy the day. He ground out his cigar on a small rock and put it in the pocket of his buckskin shirt. Then he led Sonny off the trail and into the screen of willows that lined a small creek. With a steady hand over the animal's nose, to keep Sonny from nickering a greeting, he slid the Remington revolver from his holster with the other. Silently, he kept careful watch to the east.

Through the shimmering heat waves, a human form swam into being, atop a large-eared creature, made even more ungainly in appearance by the distortion of the air. In a rough, stiff-legged gait, the unknown beast and rider covered another three hundred yards.

By then, the scout could make out the familiar blue and gold yellow stripe of a cavalry officer's uniform trousers. Why wasn't he wearing a tunic?

"Hello on the road!" Eli called out, still not showing himself.

The mule-back officer—Holten had identified the animal by then—reined in and peered toward the drooping willow branches. "Who's that?"

"How about identifying yourself first?"

"I'm Lt. Thomas Pierce, Squadron Headquarters, Fort Rawlins. Now, who the hell are you?"

"Sorry, lieutenant. It's Eli Holten, scout for the Twelfth."

"Mr. Holten! You're one of the men I'm looking for."

Holten showed himself, leading Sonny out of the marshy ground along the creek bank and through the curtain of pale, yellow-green willow leaves. Once clear, he swung into the saddle and cantered to Pierce's side. The butt-weary lieutenant was using his tunic as a saddle pad.

"What brings you after me?"

"You and Lieutenant Strickland, sir. General Corrington sent me. There's—there's been a mutiny at Fort Rawlins."

"*What!*"

"That's right, sir. A mutiny. Enlisted men from Squadron and Twelfth regimental headquarters companies banded together and attacked the post at dawn, day before yesterday. There were several killed. I don't know how many. We had an early meeting in the general's office, sir. General Corrington, Major Styles, and myself. The instigators of the mutiny pinned us

132

down in there. The general sent me out a window with orders to contact Thad Strickland and you and have you gather up what more troops you could and get to the fort quickly. He figured you could mass enough strength to retake the post, sir."

"Well, I'll be damned. Any idea who's leading this uprising?"

"N-no, sir," Pierce replied hesitantly. "One of those who was supposed to be a part of it, Trooper Greene, let me escape out the gate. Other than that, I don't know who's involved."

"All right. Strickland and that wagon train should be about three hours behind us. Can you make that mallet-head move at any other gait than that disjointed lope?"

"Only with the greatest of effort and pain."

"Now's the time to exert yourself, Pierce. We're gonna go hell for leather back to Thad and his troops."

Although slow moving, the wagon train should have covered at least fifteen miles in the eight hours since the scout left at dawn. It came as a surprise to Eli Holten to discover that they had gone nowhere near that distance. He said nothing to Pierce, only pushed on along his back trail, expecting to contact the wagons any moment. At a distance of a mile from the night camp, Holten heard the muffled reports of gunfire.

"There's trouble at the train," he informed Pierce. "We'd better circle around and come in from another direction. No telling what's going on." Briefly Eli told the cavalry officer about the difficulties with Reamer and his men, downplaying his part in it.

"Do you think they might have gotten weapons somewhere?"

"Hard to tell from here. Only, in my opinion, if they had, Thad Strickland would have made short work of them. No, I get a strong feeling there is a hell of a lot more to this. We'll ride on around to the west and see."

Half an hour later, Eli Holten and Tom Pierce lay, belly down, behind the crest of a small scarf of limestone. Through the scout's field glasses, they examined the situation below.

Some twelve Sioux warriors charged at the wagons, firing arrows and a few antique muskets. They did little damage, and Holten could identify only one wounded trooper among Strickland's command. Three civilians had been injured slightly, including one of Reamer's men. As he watched, the Indians pulled off and sat their mounts only a slight bit out of range.

"Now why in hell did they attack?" the scout mused aloud. "They're all supposed to be off on some mystic pilgrimage to bring word of a dream to the other tribes." He handed the glasses to Pierce.

"Ummm. They don't seem to be too serious about it," the young officer replied as he studied the warriors. "Or is it because there are so few of them?"

His earnest interest and ability to make valid observations impressed Eli. "No. My bet is they're only trying to pin down the wagons while more warriors come to help. Something has riled those Hunkpapas, and it has to do with the people on the train. Keep a close eye."

"Yes, sir. Uh—how did you know they were Hunkpapa?"

"By the patterns and manner they wear their feathers; also the beadwork designs on their leggings. Every tribe has different styles that no other one will wear or copy."

"I thought the Sioux were all one tribe."

"In the larger sense, yes. But there are the sub-tribes; the Yankton, Oglala, Sans Arc, Hunkpapa, Teton, Miniconjou, and the Santee, among them."

"These fellows look a lot like the Cheyenne. I was at Fort Laramie for a while. Saw a lot of Cheyenne."

"They are very close cousins to the Hunkpapa. Closer than to other Sioux tribes. Did you get that from the large amount of red color they use?"

"Y-e-s, now that you mention it, I suppose that is what made me think of it."

"The Lakota word for Cheyenne, *Sahiela,* means, 'they come red.' It's because of the red dye used in their war shirts, tipi covers, and to mark the Cheyenne arrows. They also use a lot of red war paint."

"That language sounds right practical."

"Not always," Eli assured him.

"When are we going down there?"

"Later. We'll wait for night."

Late in the afternoon, the Hunkpapa pulled off a distance and did not make another attack. A short while after that, a disturbance came from inside the circle of wagons. Brief in duration, Holten didn't even have time to focus his field glasses on the scuffle. When it ended, though, the scout discovered that his friend, Thad Strickland, and the soldiers with him, were virtual prisoners of Frank Reamer and his henchmen.

"Shit." The scout spat. "Now we've got more troubles than with the Sioux." Pierce said nothing, so Eli went on to explain. "Frank Reamer took this chance to jump Thad and his troops. They haven't been tied up, but they are as good as prisoners."

135

"Then let's get 'em out," Tom Pierce urged.

"Not a bad idea. There's only four of Reamer's men in sight. One of them must have been injured in the fighting. Five to two. That's not bad odds. Still, we'll wait for nightfall."

"We're all set to go," Myron Henshaw informed Toby Whitter. "You can head out to let Barryman know we're on the way, or ride along with us."

"I think," Whitter responded, reflecting on the drunkenness and violence abounding at Fort Rawlins, "that I'll come along with you."

"Good. We leave at dawn. Tell me again how Howard managed to bring it all off," Henshaw urged as he sprawled comfortably under the up-curved boughs of a big blackjack pine.

"It wasn't so much Howard's doing."

Quickly Whitter related once more the events of the mutiny. This time he added details about the planning conducted by Butler Bell and Vince Liscomb. He concluded by saying, "Vince Liscomb is a powerful speaker. Man, did he have those headquarters loafers standin' on their ears. I didn't go along with a lot of the crap he was puttin' out, though. I don't think many of the other fellers did, either. It was just a good excuse to raise a little hell."

"I wonder if those men realize they can be hanged for what they did." Henshaw speculated aloud.

"What?" Toby blurted in a strangled voice. "Ya mean they, *me*—we can all be hanged? Why? What for?"

"The killings for one. Anyone involved in a crime in which a murder is done, is as guilty of the death as the person who did it. And mutiny, Toby, is a crime. At least, under the Articles of War it is. For a soldier, that's the only law that counts."

"I — uh — I don't think I — w-want to go back there at all."

"What else can you do? Where can you go?"

"Away from here. That's plain as your nose. I can get different clothes, change my name. Maybe go to work for the railroads or something."

"The horse you're ridin' is branded with a *U.S.* Don't you think that would raise some questions?"

"Uh — could I swap him with one of your men?"

"I suppose so, if one of 'em is willing."

"What about clothes, too? I don't have any cash money, but I can work off what a shirt and some trousers would cost."

Henshaw smiled patronizingly. "Toby, there isn't much of what you'd call, ah, *work* that we do. You might find some sort of odd jobs to trade off for goods. Tell you what. I'll ask the boys and see."

"Would you? That would be mighty nice of you. I'd be beholden."

"No trouble. Hey, you men, listen up. Do any of you have a few chores that need doin'? Anything you would be willin' to swap a hat or a shirt for? Got a yonker here who needs a whole new outfit. He's decided the army life is not for him."

A subdued round of chuckles followed Henshaw's announcement. Then one of his hardcases raised a hand.

"I got some stitchin' needs repair on my saddle. Be worth a belt an' buckle to me t'have it done."

"Good. What else?" Henshaw asked.

"We went huntin' today," Lenny called out. "There's three mighty dirty rifles needs cleanin'. Betwixt us, we might pony up a shirt an' neckerchief."

"That's more like it. Any more?"

"I got me a pair o' pants what's too tight for me anymore," Bart Tanner supplied. "Looks like he can wear 'em. If he was to groom all the horses, might be I'd let him have 'em."

"Fine. Well, Toby, you'd better get to work."

Long after midnight, Toby Whitter finished his tasks. Exhausted, he nevertheless chose to leave immediately on a civilian-branded mount. He wanted to get far away from any connection with what was going on at Fort Rawlins. The faster he did it, the better. He chose a trail leading south and west and started off at a gentle lope.

Toby covered some twenty miles before daylight. He might have made good his escape and taken another identity with impunity. He might have.

Only he ran into five boiling mad *Wipatapi* warriors who had been sent to locate the missing families. Instead, they discovered the rotting corpses of the men, women, and children Myron Henshaw and his men had wantonly murdered.

The first arrow caught Toby Whitter in his left thigh. He let out a howl and instinctively grabbed the quivering shaft. Another arrow pierced his right shoulder. It disjointed his arm and caused it to flop uselessly into his lap. Pain and a numbing weakness forced him to slip from the saddle. In his agony, he gave no thought to reaching for his revolver, stuffed into the waistband of the wool trousers he wore. Standing beside his horse, supported by an insecure grip on his McClellan saddle, he looked frantically about, seeking his attackers in the dim, gray light.

Three Sioux braves showed themselves and walked slowly toward him. Still Toby did not draw his weapon.

They grunted and closed in. One gave a puzzled stare at the helpless white man, then raised his stone-headed war club.

A meaty plocking sound came when the pointed end of the stone buried itself to the wooden handle haft in Toby Whitter's left temple. It produced a hollow, sucking noise as the warrior wrenched it free. A syrupy flow of jellied brain tissue, blood, and spinal fluid oozed from the gaping wound.

Toby quivered like a plucked guitar string. His eyes rolled up and a crimson gush came from his mouth. Still twitching, he went slack and fell to the ground.

No one moved inside the protective circle of wagons as Yellowstone Frank Reamer harangued them. The former wagon master stood near the back end of one Conestoga and railed at the people for having trusted the army. The Sioux attack, he maintained, had been the fault of the soldiers.

"If they hadn't been along, the Indians would never have fired on us. When they did, we had to return fire in self-defense."

Not a one of the passengers, save little Patty Cramer, believed this self-serving fiction. Most of all, Hettie Dillon experienced waves of disgust and contempt. Worry and fear filled a part of her consciousness. Eli Holten had not returned by nightfall. A cold dread crowded one corner of her mind as she visualized him as captive of the savages, or worse, dead by their hands. As she stood listening to the dictums of Frank Reamer, she fought to keep her upper lip from trembling.

"So, in the morning, we reverse course and head back the proper way. This train is going to Washington Territory."

Reamer's stooges tried to raise a cheer. Their solitary voices sounded hollow and mocking in the stony silence of the majority.

"You planning to invite the Hunkpapa to join the pilgrimage?" Thad Strickland asked sarcastically. "They aren't going to disappear in a puff of smoke when the sun comes up, you know."

"Shut that mouth of yours, brass-buttons," Reamer snarled.

"What? Will those heathen savages attack us again?" a chubby, matronly settler inquired in trepidation.

"Sure as the sun comes up in the East," Lieutenant Strickland responded.

"I told you to shut your mouth!"

"If there weren't ladies present, I'd tell you what to do with your orders, Reamer."

"Pete, Issac, club him into silence!" Reamer commanded.

Solid, meaty thuds came from rifle butts striking flesh as young Lynch and the wounded Kilgore began to smash powerful blows into Thad Strickland's back, shoulders, and arms. The moment Reamer had spoken, the lieutenant had protectively covered his head. Reamer looked on with avid interest, mouth slightly agape, the pink tip of his tongue licking unconsciously at his thick lips. For a brief moment, Hettie Dillon saw

140

a blur by the extended tongue of the wagon behind Frank Reamer.

Then Eli Holten stood tight against Reamer's back, left arm around Reamer's throat, the muzzle of his cocked Remington revolver poked in the wagon master's right ear.

"Call off your dogs, Frank," the scout growled.

"Wha—"

"Call off the beating or I'll blow your fucking brains all over the prairie," Eli Holten whispered so that only the man he held around the throat could hear. Then he raised his voice.

"Pete, Issac, stop it now or I'll kill your boss." The scout's steely gaze emphasized his words as he swept over the surviving pair of Reamer's hardcases.

"One move and Frank here joins the angels."

In the darkness, from behind the rebellious crew, a Winchester hammer clicked onto full cock. "Don't reach for that hold-out gun, mister, or I'll pop your eyeballs out of your head," Tom Pierce told Drake Ferrel.

"By all the saints!" Jim Boyle exclaimed. "Sure an' it seems ye've done this little number before, Mr. Holten."

"Only this time I think I'll finish off Frank here and save us a lot of trouble."

"No! Y-you can't do that."

"Why not, Frank? All it takes is a little more pressure on the trigger. I've already taken out the slack."

"Aaah, Jesus!"

"*He* won't help you, Frank. Be nice now or I blow a hole in you big enough to drive one of these prairie schooners through. Corporal Boyle, you and the boys

141

gather up their weapons."

"Sure an' it's a pleasure, sir."

"Listen close. Those Hunkpapa are still out there. The odds are they will attack again at dawn. When the time comes, each of you who will give his parole not to turn on us will be given your guns back. You'll have a limited amount of ammunition. Use it on the Indians or die—by their hands or mine. Now, Pete, Drake, help Lieutenant Strickland over to Miss Dillon's wagon. For the rest of the night, all of you will remain under guard by the troops."

"I gotta hand it to you, Eli. You always seem to arrive at the right time."

Thad Strickland attempted a wan smile, groaned and slumped into the arms of the two ne'er-do-wells who trundled him over to Hettie's Conestoga.

Hettie bathed the lieutenant's wounds and carefully bound them while Strickland and Eli discussed plans for the anticipated sunrise attack.

"The biggest question is why they attacked at all."

"Your pal Reamer and his boys somehow got their guns back. Had them hidden. When the Sioux showed up, they took a few shots at 'em. Everything had been peaceful up until then. Damnedest part is they killed one of the warriors."

"Awh, shit. Well, we can always hope we can still parlay. In the meantime, let's get everyone rationed-out ammunition, except for Reamer and his boys, and set up a watch schedule. When it comes, I want us to be ready."

Chapter 12

"Open the gates! The wagons are coming!" shouted a somewhat less-than-sober mutineer who stood in the usual place of the sentry. "The freight wagons are here."

"Move your ass!" Butler Bell snarled at three bleary-eyed men lounging by the main gate. "Drop that fuckin' bar and swing them open. Now!"

"My ass. You think you're a fuckin' sergeant, Bell? Open the goddamned gates yourself."

A Colt .45 service revolver appeared in Bell's hand. "You wanna die sittin' down cross-legged like a fuckin' Injun? On your feet and do as you were told."

All right, all right."

Grumbling, the men came to their feet. They moved with the special lethargy of a hangover victim. A truly enormous supply of cheap whiskey and barrels of beer had been discovered in a full cellar below the sutler's store. Added to the stock on the shelves, Howard Barryman and Vince Liscomb estimated they had enough to keep fifty men continuously drunk for a month and a half.

Day or night, some group of the leaderless, shiftless soldiers started up a new segment of the week-long party. Most of them had not participated in the actual seizure of the fort, Barryman considered sourly. It made his job harder. With the wagons on the way in, these drunken roisterers only compounded his problems. If he didn't need them later, for a diversion, he'd kick them all out the gate and let them shift for themselves.

With ponderous dignity, the tall, thick gates of Fort Rawlins swung open, and the first of six gigantic freight wagons rolled in.

"Right over that way, boys," Butler Bell shouted to the teamsters, pointing toward the corral area.

"Form up at the far end of the parade ground," Howard instructed. He spotted Myron Henshaw sitting astride his mount outside the gate, keeping watch while the wagons entered. Barryman hailed him.

"Hey, Myron. Welcome to Fort Barleycorn."

Henshaw waived his hat over his head and cantered inside. He halted and dismounted outside the headquarters building. For a moment he surveyed the staggering, unkempt men who had once been good soldiers and the gambling, brawling, and other activities on the parade ground. He shook his head in dismay. Then he clasped Barryman fondly on the shoulder.

"For a time there, until I saw those gates swing wide, I thought maybe something had happened. That you didn't bring it off. This is unbelievable. A fantastic operation, carried out without a hitch. Good work,

Howard."

"Uh-thank you, Myron. Care for a little nip?"

"Would I? So long as it isn't any of that Pop Skull they sell the lower ranks."

"Oh, I got me some right fine liquor here. From the officers' private stock. How's that polish yer brick-a-brack?"

"You're one hell of an operator." Henshaw accompanied Barryman inside to General Corrington's office. The rich paneling, imported especially by the general for his enjoyment, tall, rosewood sideboard, brightly polished spitoons, and boulder-sized slab of mahogany desk made the freebooter leader do a doubletake.

"My other agent in this area reported that you handled the takeover of the fort masterfully. That led me to expect quite a lot, but this amazes me. You've come up in the world, I see."

Barryman's eyes narrowed at mention of the other operative in the area, apparently keeping watch on what he did. He brushed his irritation aside with a forced smile and waved expansively.

"As leader of this here mutiny, I thought I ought to have an office suitable to my importance. Besides, there's no sense in letting all of this go to waste. How about some brandy? Or some of these cigars?"

"Fine, fine. Yes to both."

"Sit down, Myron. I'll pour." Howard crossed to the sideboard, removed a cut-crystal decanter and dispensed two generous dollops of General Corrington's private stock into medium-sized glasses. These he carried over to where Myron sat in the large, leather-upholstered overstuffed chair.

"Your health," Howard toasted with an upward toss

of his glass.

"And yours."

"To the revolution, you should be saying, comrades," Vince Liscomb injected as he barged into the room. He glanced at a thunderstruck face of Myron Henshaw and stuck out his hand. "I'm Vince Liscomb, political officer to the liberated wage-slaves of Fort Rawlins. You must be Comrade Henshaw."

"I'm ah, Myron Henshaw, yes. What's all this political double-talk?"

Vince scowled. "It's not *double-talk* as you so rudely put it, comrade. We have struck a blow for freedom that will resound all over this mighty nation. The priviledged, the aristocratic, and the pampered bourgeoisie will be pulled down and exterminated as they deserve. The oppressed workers and starving masses will join us by the thousands. Workers of the world, unite!"

"Is he playing with a full deck?" Myron choked out.

"Vince," Howard interceded, walking over to his orator. "With me entertaining Myron, someone has to deal with the teamsters."

"Brilliant! Yes, we must do that. I'll talk with them, explain the principals of revolution, the need for a violent purging of the priviledged and the establishment of the dictatorship of the proletariat. We can join together. Form a union. The military and the teamsters. Inspired, Comrade Howard, absolutely inspired!"

"No, Vince. That's not what I mean. See they get the wagons in place at the QM warehouse and the animals unhitched and corraled. Fix 'em up for chow tonight and let 'em circulate a little. But, I'd prefer they didn't mix too much with our bunch. Too many of these yardbirds don't know what is going on. Bed 'em down and they can leave in the morning to set up a small camp away from the fort."

Vince Liscomb gave Howard Barryman a wounded look. His lower lip stuck out in a little-boy pout. "That's not showing proper revolutionary zeal, comrade. You may have to answer for this lapse in a self-criticism meeting. None of us are without error, none without revisionist flaws. We must all strive together for the millennium. I'm off now to see to the mundane needs of the carters."

"Does that answer your earlier question, Myron?" Howard inquired after Vince departed. "When we — pulled it off, the mutiny I mean, something — strange happened to Vince. He dug out this small book —" Howard made dimensions in the air with extended thumbs and forefingers. "About so-by-so. It had been printed in England about thirty years ago. He let me get a look at it, though he worried like it was some special thing, handwritten by God or something. Anyway, he began quotin' things out of it to the troops. Hell, all these guys were interested in was getting good and drunk. Damned near came to a fight. The more they ignored him, the deeper off the end he went. Now I don't even think he knows where he is."

"What do you think should be done about him?"

Barryman smiled frostily. "We can always leave him here, preaching to the know-nothings while we split out for Baja California. Let the army hang him for us. He's too far gone to remember what really happened or who was involved."

"Why not just shoot him?"

147

"Yes. Why not?"

In the stockade cells, behind the guardhouse, Gen. Frank Corrington and the two officers quartered in with him worked diligently at compounding a gritty, gray-black substance.

"I still think the plain gunpowder would do the job," Abner Styles grumbled.

"There isn't enough, Abner," General Corrington told him.

"How are we going to make up more?"

The general smiled patiently. "You never were too hot in chemistry at the Point, Abner. I remember having to tutor you every evening for the better part of one term."

"Upperclassmen," Styles moaned disgustedly. "One would think that after all these years, you would forget such twaddle."

"After all these years, I still remember my formulas. Sulphur, carbon, and potassium nitrate. Gunpowder. Simple when you know the answer."

"Where do we get the ingredients?"

"The matches provide sulphur and some nitrates. Burned wood gives us the charcoal, and those among the junior officers who are allowed out have been collecting nitrate nodes from under manure piles in the stable yard. They've been given what the enlisted men call the, ah, shit-shoveling detail. Within another day, those will be dry and we can crush, combine, and mix with our existing supply."

"Not all at once!" Abner Styles seemed horrified at the idea.

"Of course not. A small quantity, mixed fifty-fifty to

start. That should let us see if it works."

Across the passageway, Lieutenant Currey, the assistant signal officer, looked on the proceedings with growing trepidation. What if the mutineers caught them in the attempt to escape? There might be a lot of drunkenness and carousing, he considered, that could be expected. But he knew the ringleaders well enough to realize that they were dangerous. He didn't want to die on the guillotine. He also didn't want to face the consequences of a failed escape. Surely some of the men could be reasoned with. Somehow he had to make an accommodation.

Currey's guilty thoughts caused him to recoil to the back of his bunk when a voice sounded from three cells away.

"General," Captain Davis called out from down the corridor, "I think they've decided to feed us tonight. A couple of those scum are headed this way with a big open pot and a ladle. Steam's coming out of it. It could be coffee or a stew. There's more with a bread sack and some covered serving platters. Might even be meat."

"That's nice," General Corrington remarked distractedly. "We have to get these things out of sight. Cover them up. Hurry now. Everything hidden before they come in."

An eerie creaking came from outside. With a sound like the shrieks of damned souls, the heavy, weighted blade of the guillotine slowly and jerkily slid up in its slots to the top of the infernal device.

"That's it. Good—good. A little bit more," Butler Bell's voice could be heard. "Is that the way it should be, Comrade Vince?"

"It—looks all right. Let me see—aah—that's it. Put

149

in the trigger pin."

"Ease off, boys," Bell called out as he inserted the triggering device in its peg hole. "I got her stoppered off." Methodically he attached a long lanyard, designed to allow the executioner to stand well out of the way of any flying blood.

"We're ready to test her," he called expectantly to Vince Liscomb standing below the platform.

"Stick that mellon in the yoke and let her go, Comrade Bell. *Liberté — Egalité — Fraternité! Vive l'Revolution!* Pull, damnit, comrade, pull!"

With a plock, Bell yanked the trigger pin free. A sickening swish sounded as the well-oiled blade began to descend. Less than halfway down, the blade picked up a squeak, that changed to a scrape, that metamorphosed into a groan of protest. With a grinding shriek, the descending instrument of death came to a shuddering halt, wedged askew in the tracks.

"Oh shit, we've got more problems," Butler Bell complained from the scaffold.

"And thank God for that," General Corrington breathed as he looked out the cell window in fascinated horror.

Holten's conference with Lieutenant Strickland and several of the settlers lasted until well after midnight. He felt tired, aching from his slowly healing Sun Dance scars and the new punishment given him by Frank Reamer. He'd never taken so long to heal before. At least not to the point the soreness went away. Stifling a moan, he walked to the small fire Hettie had maintained and poured a cup of steaming coffee.

"There's no chance to slip outside the camp," the vivacious, tawny-haired beauty murmured in his ear.

"More's a pity. Only right now," the scout went on as he leaned back from the coffee pot, "I think I could opt for a long, restful snooze."

"Alone?"

"Not if I had my druthers."

"And you shall," Hettie announced brightly. "Come on, tired soul, and climb into the Corinthian splendor of my boudoir."

Holten pulled a shocked face. "Won't it scandalize your fellow pilgrims?"

"What do they know?" Hettie teased. "You, my handsome, sweet man need some rest, and I happen to have the softest bed on this train. Besides which, I'll be there with you."

"Who can turn down a bargain like that?" Holten downed his coffee and headed for the wagon.

Inside, he found the accommodations all they had been advertised to be. He pulled of his tall boots, buckskin shirt, and trousers and eased under a thick down comforter. Hettie lowered the wick and blew out the single lamp. Then she wriggled out of her clothing and joined the scout, her head supported by a firm goose-feather pillow.

"Ummm. This is nice," she breathed out. "And so — is this."

Hettie's hand searched and found Eli's semi-erect phallus. She squeezed and teased until it reached respectable proportions. Fully aroused, his fatigue forgotten, the scout embraced his lovely companion and began his own explorations.

Small, firm breasts yielded only slightly to his touch.

The nipples rapidly hardened and mutely cried out to be kissed. Eli readily administered their needed attentions. Hettie sighed. Then she squeaked softly as Eli's left hand found her burning mound.

Deftly his fingers parted her moist cleft and strolled tantalizingly through the slippery folds of the outer chamber. Hettie trembled. Her slight figure pressed tightly against Eli and sent shivers of secret pleasure through his bulk of bone and muscle. She eased his massive member closer and guided it to her as she swung one dainty leg over his left buttock and inched her fevered body against his solid frame.

Delectable sensations wildly stimulated the scout as he slowly entered Hettie's portal of desire. She began to wiggle forward until she had solidly impaled herself on his masterful maleness, and they joined as tightly at their groins as they did along the rest of their bodies.

"Ummm. I could stay like this forever," Hettie murmured.

"So could I. It's so — comfortable."

Holten had not moved, and he soon found he needn't. With clever contractions of a marvelous set of muscles, Hettie began a peristalsislike action that sent ripples of delirious joy through the scout's sensitive system. They remained motionless, while the contractions became more powerful and prolonged in their effect. Hettie glowed with her hidden exertion and the enormous happiness it gave her. After a long while, Eli moved slightly, thrusting the last of his goodness deep within Hettie's gyrating passage. She sighed contentedly and pressed his chest.

"Lie still now. Let me do it all."

This delightfully unusual method took longer to

build to culmination, draining them both of their sap and vitality. Arms around each other, still joined by Eli's monumental organ, they slipped into contented sleep.

The first Sioux arrow struck the side of Hettie's wagon before the scout came fully awake. Dawn presented only the thinnest of pale pink streaks on the horizon when he climbed from the Conestoga into a fullscale attack. More warriors, he saw, had arrived to join in.

In all their regalia, faces, chests, and ponies painted for war, the Hunkpapa and Oglala braves came at the sunrise-tinted, glowing tops of the wagons out of pools of darkness, riding swiftly and firing bow and rifle in wild flurries. Fortunately, most of the slugs and arrows struck wagon boxes or tore up ground. So far as the scout could tell, none of the defenders had been killed or wounded as yet. Eli turned about and took size of his defense force on that side of the circle.

Already the men and older boys, along with a few women who could shoot well, had produced weapons and began to return fire. Aiming at a dark target, against a dark background, did not make their task easier. Slowly more light seeped up from the east. Holten looked over to where Lieutenant Strickland commanded the opposite side.

Most of the marksmen on that half of the circle rested on their ready weapons and sipped coffee. So far the Sioux had not formed the usual whirling rings of warriors, riding counter to each other. Holten wondered why, until a sharp war cry sent fully twenty-five warriors racing directly toward the sector he commanded. Intent on breaking through the makeshift

153

barricades between two wagons, the Sioux did not veer off when a volley crackled out from the defenders. Howling and waving tomahawks, lances, and war clubs, they drew nearer.

To Eli Holten, it looked as though they would succeed.

Chapter 13

Somehow the battle around the wagons didn't seem to be going right. The fat, orange-hued ball of the sun had climbed an hour into the air. Three times the Sioux had charged, only to come up short of pressing their advantage of numbers. Eli Holten began to doubt that the Hunkpapa had a desire to actually finish off the defenders.

When their first charge had carried over the hastily erected barrier, the warriors inside reined to the left and began to mill about, confused, as though unprepared for reaching this strategic advantage. They whooped, counted *coup* on three startled immigrants, fired a few wild shoots, which harmed nothing, then jumped their ponies over the barricade and rode away with their companions. Holten wondered then if they had been under orders not to kill the whites. Enthusiasm and individual competitiveness might account for the sudden jump over the defenses. The second charge, which also stopped short of total engagement, added weight to his contemplations.

After all, one brave had been killed, according to Thad Strickland, and one of Reamer's men had also been eliminated. The sides remained even on that. A few wounds had been received among both opponents in earlier fighting, yet no concerted effort to do more damage since. Admiration for the Hunkpapa leader rose in Holten's mind. It would be difficult to maintain such iron control over Sioux warriors for long. That he had apparently been able to do so thus far made him a remarkable man. The closing-in thunder of unseen hoofbeats brought the scout out of his speculations. One or the other faction would be receiving reinforcements. Somehow he didn't think it would be the beleagured wagon train.

The third charge confirmed this for him as he recognized the markings of Oglala patterns on arrows fired into the defensive circle. Likewise, several of the newly arrived braves wore distinctive designs on shields and the breasts of their ponies. In the midst of the wild swirl, Eli thought he recognized the face of Gray Beaver of the Quill Workers. It might be, he considered, time to call for a parley.

"Thad," the scout called to his friend. "Have everyone hold their fire. I want to see if we can have a powwow."

"What?" Lt. Strickland snapped back. "Those warriors have fire in the eyes, Eli."

"That may be," Holten answered. "But have you noticed how poor their aim is?"

That fact had not been lost on the experienced cavalry officer. "What do you think is behind that?"

"For some reason, their hearts aren't in finishing us off. They just might be putting on a show for the sake of honor."

"And scaring the trousers right off these pilgrims," Thad added. "Who's to go talk with them?"

Eli considered that a moment. In light of the touchy situation with Reamer and his surviving men, he felt it wise to keep someone in authority inside the ring of wagons. His language facility would be needed, so that left Strickland.

"Corporal Boyle and I will go. You keep an eye on Reamer. What we don't need now is another dead Indian." Eli turned and started toward where he had left his Morgan.

"Corporal Boyle, accompany Mr. Holten, if you will," Lieutenant Strickland called out.

"Do you think I should come along?" Lieutenant Pierce offered.

"Hummm. It might not hurt. They've seen Thad before. Another officer might get them thinking there's more troops on the way. We could always try that as a bluff. Get your, ah, no, get Thad's horse. That mule you were riding won't quite do. We want the Sioux relaxed but not laughing their heads off."

Tom Pierce frowned over this. "What's behind that?"

"Most Indians consider mules quite tasty for a meal, fine for carrying large loads, but altogether ridiculous to ride. Saddle up and let's go."

A rustle of skirts interrupted Eli's work at tightening his cinch. Hettie came to him, face furrowed with worry lines.

"Please be careful, Eli. Isn't it terribly dangerous trusting those savages to honor a flag of truce?"

"Not at all. They understand what it means. Matter of fact, the tribes have been usin' white feathers for the same purpose for a long time before the white man came. And they're honest. Scrupulously so. If they give their word to a parley, they won't bother with back-shooting or an ambush along the way."

"Even so — I can't help but worry."

"Relax. I'm not even sure we can set this up."

Hettie produced a wan smile. "Come back to me in one piece, Eli dear."

If anything, the drunken men were becoming worse, General Corrington concluded as he watched out the small window of his cell. This one had lasted all through the night. While most of the men at the fort participated, some did not. They busied themselves loading items out of the quartermaster stores into tall freight wagons. That activity had stopped about two hours ago. The general thought it time for the test.

"Careful now," he cautioned. "Tamp it down carefully in the casing."

His cell mates worked on one of the spare cartridges obtained from the unfortunate Lieutenant Abel. They poured a mixture of regular black powder and the homemade explosive into the open end of the brass .45 shell. When finished, they would tamp a paper wad over the powder and insert the round in one chamber of a Colt cylinder.

"That's it," General Corrington told them. "Now compress that paper over the top."

For this experiment, the casing had been loaded with less than a quarter of the usual amount of powder. The last thing the hopeful officers wanted was an explosion loud enough to betray their plan. Out on the parade, as the escape committee completed its efforts, three drunken ex-troopers argued about their marksmanship and began to make wild bets. To prove their exaggerated claims, they agreed to set up some playing cards as targets and shoot out the spots. Similar contests had been held before, and a glitter of broken bottles and shreds of pasteboard littered the ground. Silently the general urged them on. Their activity would help mask any sound from the guardhouse.

While the noisy preparations continued for the shooting contest, General Corrington took the blank cartridge and inserted it into one chamber of a Colt cylinder. "This could be a bit on the dangerous side," the commander of Fort Rawlins remarked unnecessarily. "Everyone stand clear."

Corrington fitted his pocket knife into a shallow notch in the mud caulking of the wall. Next he rested the live primer of the cartridge on the sharp tip of the blade. He hefted a boot and prepared to smash it against the front of the cylinder.

"You'd better protect your hand with my tunic, sir," Abner Styles suggested, removing his uniform coat.

"Good idea, Abner." Quickly the general wrapped the tunic around his left hand and arm. Then he clutched the cylinder firmly and swung back the boot. "Well, here goes."

Firing erupted outside as the drunks blazed away at their small targets. Raucous shouts came from the trio of inebriates.

"Yeeee-ha! I'm gonna pop out every spot," one declared.

"Awh, hell. You can' even see 'em from here. How'er you gonna do that?"

Another shot sounded, and General Corrington swung the boot. A flash of fire, a dull boom, and a small, sulphurous cloud formed in the cell. Its detonation blended in with the bark of six-guns from outside.

"D'you hear that?" one sharp-eared drunk slurred.

"What?"

"Unnh — nothin'. An echo, I suppose."

Frank Corrington shook his stinging left hand. A light, cherry red blushed the skin. "That smarted like hell, but it worked. By God it really worked. I think we can blow a hole in this wall any time we want. Tell the others to get ready. Any luck on picking cell door locks?"

"Yes," Styles answered him. "Besides ours, there's three cells that can be opened."

"Then let's get that pocket dug out large enough to hold all the powder we've got."

In his bunk across the way, Lt. Brian Currey awakened with a start at the sound of the dull explosion. Immediately he began to bite on one well-chewed fingernail. His nightmare had come true. The crudely made gunpowder worked. He had to do something before it was too late. While the furtive activity went on around him, he watched with frightened eyes. An hour after dawn food smells came from the headquarters mess hall and reminded the prisoners of the scant few meals they had been given since the mutiny.

As if by afterthought, once the majority of the rebellious soldiers had entered and left the dining room, three of the mutineers came from the rear door, laden down with large food containers. By the time

160

they reached the guardhouse, Currey had made up his mind what he had to do.

When the men bearing the thin oatmeal gruel and weak coffee reached the cell, Currey sidled up to them and whispered urgently.

"I've got something important to tell Barryman. About an escape plan. Do something to get me out to him without anyone becoming suspicious."

"Huh?" a blank-faced hangover sufferer grunted.

"I have to talk to Howard Barryman," Currey breathed out in a tense rush. "It's important. Get me to him without anyone here knowing."

"Uh—yeah. Yeah, sure."

Panic and a sense of failure chilled Lt. Brian Currey. For a moment, after the mess detail moved on, he stood mechanically shoveling the tasteless breakfast into his mouth. What would happen if he had not convinced that lout? Black despair settled over him, and he cursed the day he had agreed to attend West Point.

"They'll talk with us," Eli announced as he stepped back inside the circle of wagons. "Their leader, Broken Paw, seemed right eager to do it. Pierce, Boyle, mount up. We're to meet with Broken Paw and two others up by those pines."

Ten minutes later, the peace party dismounted, and Holten spread a blanket. He masked his surprise at finding Iron Claw present, along with Broken Paw and, as he had suspected, Gray Beaver. Broken Bow produced a pipe and it went its ritual rounds. Gray Beaver spoke first.

"Tall Bear, are you *tonwaya* of these treacherous whites?"

"Yes and no," the scout replied. "I am with the soldiers. We are taking these whites out of your country. We do not want them there while you spread the word of your new medicine to the other tribes. I am scouting for them on the way back to Fort Rawlins."

"That is good," Gray Beaver agreed.

"Even so, they fired on us. Killed my cousin, Crooked Nose," Broken Paw inserted aggressively.

"Those men who shot at you are bad to everyone. They tried to use guns against the army. We are taking them to the fort to be punished. Also, you or one of your braves killed one of them. You are even on that."

Silence held a long minute. "That is so," Broken Bow said. "We are many now. We could wipe you all out."

"You speak the truth, Broken Paw," Holten replied. "But—do you really want to do that?"

Again a long quiet ensued while the Sioux considered this probe.

"Prisoners Markham, Currey, and Linderman, step to the front of your cells," Butler Bell declared an hour after the message had been sent. "You are being summoned for trial for your many offenses against the people."

Brian Currey nearly wept with relief. His gamble had paid off. No one would suspect. With a light heart, which he found difficult to disguise from his fellow officers, he walked out into the corridor and allowed manacles to be put on his wrists. He wanted to shout with relief. The armed escort took them from the guardhouse and across the parade to the headquarters building.

"In there," a rough-handed mutineer commanded as he directed each of the officers to a different room. "You will be questioned and have a chance to talk with the man who will defend you."

Once inside the indicated office, Lt. Brian Currey found himself facing Howard Barryman and Vince Liscomb. They sneered at the nervous young lieutenant and let him stand a long while before speaking.

"What is this dangerous plot you have to tell us about?" Liscomb began.

"It's—I want you to understand that I am doing this for the best interests of my fellow officers."

"Of course you are," Howard Barryman purred. "Go on."

"Well, General Corrington and some others have created enough gunpowder to blow out a section of wall. They plan to do it tonight and we're all to escape. I—I thought you ought to know."

"Interesting. Don't you find that interesting, Vince?" Liscomb glowered. "Yes, comrade, I do. Tell us more, ah, Currey, isn't it?"

"Y-yes. I'm Brian Currey. It's like this. Someone left four spare magazines in Abel's pouches. He had OOD when the fort was seized. They were loaded. When the general found this out, he started figuring out how to make more powder. His ideas worked. He tested it this morning around sunup. Now they're going to blow out a part of the wall."

"You are sure of this?" Barryman's voice had gone hard and cold.

"Yes."

"Why did you think we should know this?"

"Uh—I've had time to think since, ah, going into the stockade. I'm not all so certain now that the, ah, way things were before had been entirely fair."

"You really are an officer?" On Currey's assurance he was, Barryman went on. "How is it then that you can have this miraculous change of heart?"

"I—I was never cut out to be in the army. Believe me, I wasn't. I abhore violence, guns make me almost sick with fear. Men being subjected to dehumanizing regimentation—" Currey caught the glower on Liscomb's face and hurried to clarify his remark, "without a proper reason, is evil. The—the punishments that can be, and have been, meted out here horrify me. Bloody and brutal."

"Then why did you ever decide to get that fancy ring?" Liscomb injected with a contemptuous gesture toward Currey's West Point class ring.

"I—It was my family's idea. A tradition. I wanted no part of it. But—well, you see—I couldn't let them down, don't you see? I—I would have been disowned. Left penniless."

"A goddamned aristocrat," Liscomb snarled. "We ought to put him against the wall and shoot him with those other two."

"No! No, *please*. I've aided you with information on this escape. I—can help you more in the future."

Liscomb started to make a hot reply, only to cut it off when Barryman raised a hand to silence him. "Oh? Tell us more," Howard encouraged in a syrupy voice.

"I don't know anything more about the escape, or anything else right now. Except, Major Styles, the adjutant, Major Canfield, and the three senior captains are in on it. But, I can hear things. Pass them along to you. I—I don't want to die. Not here, not this way. I can be very useful to you, to your cause."

"I still say shoot this aristo bastard, or *ziiiit*! Off with his head!"

Tears began to leak from Brian Currey's eyes. His knees went weak, and he feared he might vomit on the dark bearskin rug on General Corrington's office floor.

"Tell me, Brian, how useful can you be?"

"I'll do anything. Anything at all you assign me."

"I like willing workers, don't you, Vince? Would you join us in our overthrow of the army brass?"

"Uh—I—never thought of that before. I—well—if I had to, yes, I would join you." Currey took a deep breath. Now that he had said it, he felt a great deal better.

Liscomb's voice rang with incredulity. "You mean you *believe* this little asshole?"

"I do. I think he's so scared for his own skin right now that if you wanted to drop his drawers and bend him over, he'd let you play rumpty-dumpty in his backside to your heart's content. Send men to search the prisoners. Find that gunpowder and any other contraband they might have. I want it brought here. As to General Fat Ass Corrington, I think he needs a taste of what he gave Whitter and Thorne. Arrange for it. Have 'em lashed to wagon wheels within the hour."

Chapter 14

Iron Claw leaned forward and spoke earnestly. "As you were to Two Bulls, so are you to me, Tall Bear. I look on you as a son. Gray Beaver and ten *Wipatapi* slipped away from the eyes of the pony-soldiers to come help a wronged brother. So did I and some of our warriors. We find you here. At first this makes our hearts heavy. Is this the start of the final battle predicted in Kicking Elk's dream at the *winwanyag waci?* Have you taken the side of the *wasicun* over the Dakota?

"Even so, Gray Beaver and I counsel that we do not overwhelm these rolling wood lodges so quickly. That we wait and learn what is in the heart of Tall Bear. It is why we are willing to counsel with you and hear what are your thoughts."

"And why your warriors did not kill the whites in the wagons, eh, Father?" Eli Holten asked back to Iron Claw.

The three Sioux leaders nodded gravely. "Killing

only breeds more killing, Tall Bear," Gray Beaver offered.

Holten breathed out gustily. "That is so, Gray Beaver. You are known as a man of peace, a man of thoughts and words. Everyone seeks the beautiful porcupine quill work of the *Wipatapi* to decorate many things with. Such wonders can come only from people who are at peace in their hearts. Yet you bring your braves here to make war?"

"To see justice done," Gray Beaver responded.

"As did I," Iron Claw added.

"Then we three are alike." Quickly Holten reviewed the circumstances of Yellowstone Frank Reamer's attack on Broken Bow's family, emphasized that the army, in the person of Thad Strickland, placed Reamer and his men under arrest. He concluded with their sincere wish that peace be resumed and an assurance that Reamer would be brought to justice.

A faint smile flickered at the corners of Broken Bow's stern mouth. "We saw you, Tall Bear, and this pony-soldier chief, sneak into the camp last night. Saw you put your guns on the men who shot my cousin. It is good. But we ask, where are the other soldiers that they do not ride to this place, scatter my small family and join the wagons? What is the answer to that?"

Holten gave him a wry grin. "That there are no other soldiers. All but a few are out in the field, looking for the *Dakota* and *Śahiela*. All of the bands have wandered far from their homes to carry the message of the Sun Dance. This is not as the treaty allows. Those who have signed must go to their homes. Those who live outside the agreement need safe conduct so as not to frighten peaceful whites living along the way. Such a job takes many soldiers. As I said before, we are here to take this wagon train away from your land so there will be continued peace between us. I have spoken."

"These are good words that Tall Bear speaks. To seal our peace and further proclaim our friendship, I will send my ten warriors along with the rolling wood lodges to the place of the soldier village," Gray Beaver offered.

"That is generous, Gray Beaver," Eli declared. "We welcome you to ride beside our soldiers as brothers."

"What's all of this about?" Tom Pierce whispered. Holten translated the gist of their discussion. The young lieutenant's eyes widened, and he expressed his discomfort with this arrangement. "Isn't there some other way?"

"Not and keep these Sioux happy with us. We have to show them we trust them and accept their word as bond."

"I, too, will send ten of my people along with Tall Bear. My heart will be light when they return to me and say that the rolling wood lodges are gone from our land, and that those who killed my cousin, Crooked Nose, have had their necks made longer by the rope."

"You are a generous man, Broken Bow," Holten replied. "He's sending ten Hunkpapa warriors along to keep us honest," the scout translated to Pierce.

"Do—do you do things like this out here all the time?"

"Barter makes the world go around, Mr. Pierce. Beyond the walls of Fort Rawlins, regimental and squadron orders and regulations often have no relationship with reality. Maintaining the peace frequently requires something entirely different from what is decreed from above. The Sioux have no conception of the Department of Dakota or what its authority represents. They couldn't care less about anything written on paper. What works is what's done."

"Well, as a staff officer type, I must admit I have apparently led a sheltered life."

Holten smiled. "Being in the field will be good for you, then. Ask our friend, Thad Strickland, about it. Most of the hide-bound directives tend to stick in the craw of any regimental officer in the field. Keep in mind that there's no such thing as a set way out here, and you'll survive to tell your grandchildren about it."

"It is agreeable to your pony-soldier chiefs?" Iron Claw inquired.

"Yes. We will be honored to ride with the Hunkpapa and the Quill Workers," Holten responded.

Abruptly, Tom Pierce began to laugh. "Wait until we tell Reamer about this," he gusted out.

"This hub hurts like all the fiends of hell," General Corrington grunted in a pained whisper to Abner Styles, who hung at his side.

Hot circles of pain tormented the middle of their backs where the wood and metal of the hubs dug in. Fiery shafts of agony lanced out from their shoulder joints. The upward shoots brought on incredible waves of sick-headache misery, while those that radiated downward joined similar assaults on their nervous systems from the region of their hip joints.

"The bitch of it is that you can't move and spread the pain out a little," Major Styles said. "Did we *actually* order such punishment for the men under us?"

"Having second thoughts, Abner?"

"No. Only making an observation. No wonder those who had a spell on the wheel either reenlisted and became outstanding soldiers or got out of the army at the first opportunity. A man can't experience this—this torment and retain a neutral attitude."

"Stop that talkin' over there," a rough voice growled.

"Are we going to be taken down for the night?" the general inquired.

"Naw. Barryman thought it would do you some good to hang there until dawn."

"They crucified Jesus in less than six hours on the cross," Corrington responded. "I thought Barryman was hot to see our heads chopped off."

"Not him. It's that *Comrade* Vince feller. Barryman'd had his way all you officers would have had your brains blown out a long time ago."

"How considerate of him." The commander of Fort Rawlins could not resist the note of sarcasm. "But, I gather you don't much care for Vince Liscomb?"

"Nope. Ain't many of us do. All we wanted was to get out from under the orders of routine for a while. Never figured on this. Too many men gettin' drunk, too many workin' at strippin' everythin' out of the quartermaster warehouse. An' too damned much of this lecturin' by Liscomb.

"Shit! We're all supposed to call each other *comrade*. That or *citoyen,* what ever the hell that means. Bunch of foreign flimflam, you ask me. We don't want to overthrow anything, let alone the government. I tell you, Liscomb is plumb crazy." By this time, the weaponless sentry had walked over close to the punishment wheels.

"Then why do you put up with—all of this?"

170

" 'Cause, Barryman an' them's what's followin' him an' Liscomb has got all the guns. They were quick enough in passin' 'em out when they wanted to take the fort. Just as fast at gatherin' 'em all in, too. Wouldn't do for us common so'jers to have guns, Liscomb said. It wasn't safe."

"Safe for whom, I wonder?" the general prompted.

"Huh! Don't take no smart man to figure that one out, gen'ral. The boys is sorta gettin' fed up with all the bossiness and airs Liscomb is takin' on. An' that feller Henshaw, what came with the wagons. He an' Barryman are tight as ticks. To hear them talk, you'd think the rest of us is less than something that floated to the top of an outhouse pit. The more that hears that sort of thing, the more wants to maybe put a stop to all this. Hand the fort back to you and those what's properly in charge, don't ya see?"

"You—ah, you mean that some of you men actually feel that way?"

"Sure, but it don't amount to a hill of beans. So long as Barryman and Liscomb and their cronies have all of the guns, there ain't a lot we can do about it. Why, just the other day, one o' my good friends got shot down like a dog for complainin' aloud over Liscomb spoutin' all this 'tide of the future' an' 'one world social order' blather. Man without a gun can't protect himself from that kind o' fan-a-fanatic."

General Corrington began to tingle with excitement. "Would you—ah, I mean, would some of those who felt this way be willing to help us? To do something to get the fort back from Barryman and Liscomb?"

A long, tense moment passed while the soldier contemplated this. "Wu—l—l—I suppose it could be

171

asked around. All on the quiet side, of course."

"Thank you. That — that is the most promising thing I've heard around here in a while."

"In the meantime," Abner Styles asked, "couldn't you do something about seeing that we're cut down for the night? We can't hold our weight up here for long. When we sag, it will close off our lungs and we'll suffocate."

"Hummm. Sounds reasonable it could happen like that. I'll mention it to Butler Bell. He's the, ah, revolutionary counsel's executioner. It'd be up to him an' Barryman."

After the sentry drifted away in search of Bell, the general spoke something else he had in mind. "Who do you suppose betrayed our plan to escape?"

Abner Styles chewed on it for a while. "Only one I can think of is Lieutenant Currey. Brian Currey. There's talk around Squadron HQ that he's a sissy. Something dangerous like this could put that kind over the edge."

"Anything that might point definitely at it?"

"Ummm. There was that young trooper, a real baby-faced boy fresh out of some farm, who wanted a transfer not long ago. He wouldn't give a reason, but he sure came on as desperate to get away from Fort Rawlins. He was a clerk, assigned to the signal office."

"Currey's section," the general declared. "Yes. It makes you wonder. What could Currey expect to get out of betraying us?"

"To save his delicate skin. Frank, if he's inclined toward that sort of life, he'd be easy to manipulate by someone shrewd as Barryman. It could be a threat to make his sexual tastes public. Or just plain terror.

Sissies are sort of cowardly."

"The Greek hoplites and the Spartans were supposed to be composed of that sort, and they fielded some mighty fierce soldiers."

"Sure. Only the Greeks condoned such things. Here and now the sissies try to keep it a deep, dark secret. As things stand, I'd have to put my bet on Currey."

Corrington sighed sadly. "I'm sorry to say I must also. I pity that boy when this is all over. Someone is sure to want revenge."

"You're thinkin' of higher headquarters?"

"No. I've got Eli Holten in mind."

Eli Holten and Hettie Dillon sat on the far side of a high swale, beyond where the night camp had been made for the mixed company with the wagon train. Bemused by the utter beauty, they watched the sun slide out of sight below the western horizon.

Surrounded by a splendorous array of pastel colors, the giant red-orange ball seemed to hesitate a long, sighing moment, as though reluctant to leave the magnificent vista of the sprawling prairie it had illuminated. Its dramatic departure put the amorous couple into a pensive mood.

"Thad, Tom and I have to lay plans on what to do when we reach Fort Rawlins."

Hettie put an anxious hand on the scout's arm. "Will there be fighting?"

"Unless they give up peaceably, there will. I wonder how the Sioux are going to take that, if we have to battle our way into the fort?"

The afterglow spread bars of soft rose, powder blue,

173

and fading green along the roll of the plains and up in stippled layers to the lengthening dome of night. Hettie moved closer to Eli and rested her head of springy brown sausage curls in the notch of his collar bone.

"We are going to push hard for the next two days. That'll bring us in close to the fort. Reamer and his men will be made captive and held with the train while the rest of us ride ahead to reconnoiter the fort. That show of force might be enough to topple this mutiny."

"Oh, I hope so. I'm—frankly I'm worried Eli. Reamer and his men are a known threat. We have twenty Sioux warriors riding right in with the soldiers, and we're headed toward a mutinous force of unknown numbers. I can't think of a more perilous situation."

Eli put his arm around Hettie's shoulders. "How about five thousand or so angry Sioux warriors boiling over the frontier, killing every white man, woman, and child they encounter? That's what it could mean if we fail to keep this wandering of theirs under control and prevent any incidents that could lead to war. Likewise, we have to get the fort back in proper hands for the same reason. As a base of operations to control Indian movements, Fort Rawlins is ideally situated. Better, in fact, than any other installation in the Departments of Dakota or Wyoming."

"Let's not talk strategy now, dearest," Hettie said. "I didn't drag you out here to get myself scared thinking about an uprising. I planned to get—something else."

Holten pulled her lips to his, and they killed worry with mounting passion. Never slow to rise to any occasion, his long, sensitive organ began to fill and grow erect. His loins throbbed with energy as he escalated toward shimmering excitement. When they parted, Eli held Hettie at arm's length and peered into her fathomless eyes.

"We won't have much opportunity to, ah, be together after tonight, Hettie. Taking back the fort and settling this problem with the migrating tribes is going to occupy a lot of time."

"Then let's make the most of it. That setting sun is enchanting. I've never made love under a sunset sky before. Hurry, let's fill our heads with all those colors like the heavens."

Clothing went several directions and soon the buffalo grass and wild sage concealed the soft moans and pleasurable coos. The scout entered her eagerly, his long, upwardly curved organ driving far into her tight passage, stroking its sensitive length along warm, moist walls that quivered with their own titillation. He held to a languorous, rocking stroke that sent shivers up Hettie's spine and small jolts of electric delight playing over his bare skin. The soothing breeze fanned their ardor, and they gave into the demands of sweet delirium.

Stars began to appear and wheeled across the sky as they rocked to the primitive rhythm of creation. Hettie nearly cried out and tightly clasped Eli's bare buttocks in an attempt to ingest more of his mighty shaft. Slowly the tempo of their tidal surging increased and their moans grew louder.

"Oooh! Aaaaah! Eeeee-li! Eeee-li!" Hettie wailed as the stallion-sized rod of silken flesh probed to her utmost depths. She quivered and held him tightly as his lips found first one of her erect nipples, then the other. His beat grew faster, and he began to swivel his hips in an enthralling manner that drove them both into a frenzy of pleasure.

Slowly at first, then with demanding rapidity, the joyful couple scrambled up the steep incline. Each ecstatic fraction of an instant became indelibly recorded on their screaming senses, as they blended their souls in the race to the sublime culmination. In a quivering rush of mutual release, they exploded into a celestial oblivion that left them drained and limp.

Whatever fate the morrow would bring to him, the scout no longer contemplated it. Only the glory of their sensual *now* filled his mind with a rosy fog of healing rapture.

Chapter 15

Another grueling day awaited General Corrington and his adjutant. They sweated and groaned in the sun, arm and leg joints inflamed with nearly unbearable pain. The relentless sun burned their naked torsos, then raised agonizing blisters that burst to reveal tender, unprotected flesh, which the flies swarmed to and gorged upon. By nightfall, when at last Butler Bell ordered them cut down, they remained barely rational and hardly conscious. They hadn't even the strength to protest when told that still another ten hours of torment awaited them on the morrow.

Within an hour after breakfast, the bored, listless troops had gathered in knots to watch other, more active men load a pair of small galloper cannon onto a freight wagon. A hot sun beat down and gave a stark appearance to the smooth sand of the parade ground. Only a few — those not already in a drunken stupor from early morning excess — paid any attention when the two debilitated officers were dragged from the stockade and attached to the punishment wheels. Several shouted insults and snickered at the discomfort of the commanding general and his adjutant. Time burned into their naked flesh like the cruel fibers of the hemp ropes that held them in place.

Albert Styles lost consciousness in mid-afternoon. He hung limply, face a deep scarlet, lips nearly purple. It took all the energy he could muster in Frank Corrington to yell out loudly enough for one of those in charge to hear him.

"Cut him down, damn you. He'll die if you don't."

"Oh, what's the matter, General Fat Ass?" Howard Barryman murmured in a nasty voice near Corrington's ear. A ripple of drunken laughter came from those standing nearby. "He couldn't take it, is that what you're complaining about?"

"Let him down," the general croaked. "He's not even suffering now. Out cold. Do it, you goddamned animal!"

"Now, now. Such harsh language," Barryman said. "Why, one would almost think you were in charge here instead of me. But then, we would be deprived of our little show if Major Styles failed to hold together for the guillotine. Greene, Lymon, cut the major down. Splash some water on him. When he comes around, back up on the wheel again."

"I'm putting Nathanial Pritchard in charge of you civilians on the train," Thad Strickland informed the gathered immigrants early the next morning. "Two troopers are staying behind to guard Frank Reamer and his men. They are to be kept bound and isolated from everyone else. The rest of us have to make haste to Fort Rawlins. As I'm no doubt sure you know there has been a mutiny there. It is our intention to quell it and return to you. In the event we are unable to effect a conclusion of this unfortunate situation at once, we will escort you all to the town of Eagle Pass. There you can remain safely until the Indian problem is resolved. Ezra Grimes will accompany the expedition to the fort, in charge of those men who have volunteered. I needn't tell you how grateful we are to all of you who have offered to help. That's everything for now. Everyone remain calm and do what is necessary, and we'll come out of this in good order."

"I'm not so sure of that," an elder member of the train's occupants complained.

"Well, *I* can certainly assure you," Zonah Prichard said and sniffed, "that everything is in good hands. My husband is an experienced teamster. He can take care of our wagons well enough. As for the soldiers, the lieutenant certainly handled those savages cleverly a while back. I say we do our all to help out now."

"I agree, Zonah," Dulcia Grimes added. "We owe our lives to Mr. Holten, Lieutenant Strickland, and these fine boys. Now we should do what we can to ease *their* burden."

"What's gonna happen to Cap'n Reamer?" the elderly man snapped back.

"He and his men are going to be tried for murder. They shot that Sioux warrior. Also for several other criminal counts in violation of the Red Cloud Treaty. No more questions, please. We really must be on our way to Fort Rawlins. Corporal Boyle, mount the men."

"Pre-pare to mount! Mount!"

"Column of twos to the left." Strickland commanded.

"Ma-rch! Mr. Holten, would you be so kind as to lead out and scout our way?" Strickland concluded as the creak of leather and jingle of metal rings and chain accompanied the column's movement.

Ahead of the small force by two miles, Eli Holten saw the captive fort first. From the outside little seemed to be disturbed. Only the keen eye of the scout made out the discrepancies. The stars and stripes did not fly, as usual, from the tall staff outside headquarters. No sentries paced the walls. Only a thin wisp of smoke rose from inside the palisades. No work was getting done. He heard things, though.

Drunken shouts and barks of laughter came from inside buildings and on the parade ground. An occasional random shot blasted the late afternoon heat and rolled lonesomely across the prairie. By his judgement, Tom Pierce's description of the situation had been entirely accurate. He turned his mount and hastened back to join the column.

Two officers, an NCO, three troopers, twenty Sioux warriors painted for war, and a dozen civilian volunteers made a disturbingly odd sight. The motley, though blatantly hostile column failed, however, to make much impression on the conquerors of Fort Rawlins. When they rode to within fifty yards of the captured post and halted, a drunkenly weaving sentry pulled himself from the shadows where he had been loafing and raised his rifle.

"Halt. Who are you?"

"This is Lt. Thaddeus Strickland, Twelfth U.S. Cavalry from Fort Rawlins."

The intoxicated guard sniggered. "There ain't no Fort Rawlins anymore. This here is *Egalité* City. State yer business."

"You men are in serious violation of the Articles of War. I order you to lay down your arms and surrender control of the fort back to lawfully constituted authority."

"Go suck an egg, sonny. This is our place now, an' we ain't gonna give it up."

"This is your last chance. Free any prisoners you hold and throw down your weapons. Otherwise we will attack!"

"Fuck off, Strickland, yer yellin's givin' me a headache."

"Is that you, Trooper Bell?" Thad demanded of a stoutly built man who appeared beside the sentry.

"Sure as hell is. We got the fort, we got the general, and we got the whole shootin' match. Now haul yer butts outta here before we blow 'em off you."

"There will be no mercy shown from this point on, Bell. Corporal," Strickland said over his shoulder to Jim Boyle. "I think we'll use the carbines this time."

"Pre-pare to draw carbines."

"Draw your carbines."

"Draw carbines!" Boyle repeated.

"In a line, as skirmishers. March!"

Sloppily, the Sioux warriors not fully understanding what was going on, the column formed up in an irregular line, facing the ramparts of Fort Rawlins. The braves thought this most unusual and muttered among themselves about the vagaries of the white men.

"Trumpeter Smith, sound the 'Charge.' "

Although not entirely in tune — the company's trumpeter sergeant had gone on after the bulk of the Sioux—the staccato notes of the awesome bugle call sounded crisply over the sod.

Instantly, thirty-six sets of hoofs pounded into the soil and strained to leap forward. A moment after the long file went into motion, a puff of smoke billowed from the wall.

Right upon its heels came the sharp bark of a six pound galloper. The small projectile whined through the air and struck behind the charging force. Its minute charge detonated, and two horses screamed in agony from shrapnel wounds. Another muzzle belched greasy puffs, and two Sioux warriors catapulted off their mounts and lay bleeding and kicking out their lives on the hard ground.

"They're using the artillery," Strickland said aloud and added a curse. "We'll have to pull back. Hold up men! Hold up here! Trumpeter, sound 'Recall.' "

A shamefaced group came back from the failed attempt. For a while they said nothing after riding into the ring of wagons. At last, Eli Holten rose in his stirrups and waved his arms for attention.

"The force that captured the fort is large and powerful. They have at least two cannons mounted on the wall. If they have enough willing gunners to cooperate, they can slaughter us all.

"We'll escort you to Eagle Pass. The women and children will be safe there. Then we have to devise a means of entering the fort. Make ready to roll. We'll move out in fifteen minutes."

A new light of hope glowed deep in Frank Corrington's eyes. Despite his agony on the wagon wheel, he had heard the challenging voices, the fine, clear command tones of Thad Strickland and the cannon shots that had ended the confrontation. Pierce had made it! Somehow that knowledge alone buoyed the general's spirits. He rolled his head so he could look at Abner Styles.

"Y-e-s," Styles forced out. "I heard it too. We—we've a chance, Frank."

"And don't you forget that," the commander of Fort Rawlins demanded with a bit of his old forcefulness. "If anyone can put a stop to this, it's Eli Holten and Thad Strickland. We've got more than a chance. It's a sure thing, now."

The fine gravel of the parade ground crunched under foot as Howard Barryman approached the crudely crucified officers. He had a smug grin on his face and a fire of madness in his eyes. He halted a short distance from the wagon wheels and stood, fists on hips, to appraise his victims.

"So much for that. A couple of shots from those gallopers and we ran your rescuers off. Hell, they won't stop until they reach Fort Abraham Lincoln. By that time, we'll be long gone. Oh, by the way—" Barryman feigned ingenuousness, as though the thought had only then come to him. "You'll be glad to know this, I'm sure. The guillotine is working fine now. We enlarged the guide-slots and greased the guides with pig fat. No more troubles. So the date of your execution has been finalized. You will lose your heads the day after tomorrow at sundown. A fitting time, no?"

With typical frontier hospitality and genuine pioneer compassion, the people of Eagle Pass welcomed the refugees. A corral at the livery was made available, at no cost, for their draft animals and another for riding stock. The wagons could be forgotten for a while, the generous townspeople declared. Real beds, under civilized roofs, would be provided for their convenience. Among those crowding around to offer assistance, Eli Holten noticed, with a twinge of conscience, was the face of Constance Albright.

"Uh," he hesitantly started to explain to Thad Strickland and Hettie Dillon, "there's, ah, something I have to take care of." He guided Sonny out of the crush of immigrants and townfolk and walked the big Morgan over to a tie-rail in front of the hotel.

He entered and waited with mild, but growing, trepidation, until Constance entered and ascended the stairs to her room. Fingering his hatband with the nervous gesture of a backward schoolboy, he followed a minute later. Constance answered his first knock.

"Uh, Connie, it's me, Eli."

She opened the door slowly. Could it be reluctantly? Eli worried as he studied her face. Hardly alight with welcoming passion, he considered. Her smile, when it came, seemed forced.

"Well, come on in, Eli. I didn't expect you."

With growing unease, Eli entered the room and looked at the familiar, institutional furniture and the large maple armoire, stuffed to overflowing with creations made from Constance Albright's designs. He wanted to ignore all of that, to reach out and draw the lovely young woman to him for a long, fiery kiss. Memories of his amorous hours with Hettie Dillon intruded. His face flamed.

"I saw the look she gave you," Constance began coolly.

"Who? What? Where?"

"Don't try to play innocent, Eli. We women know. I'm talking about that overblown female temptress on the wagon train."

"Y-you mean, Hettie? Uh, she's hardly what you could describe as overblown. A bit on the petite side, I would say."

"And of course you had ample opportunity to find out for yourself." A catty edge had entered Constance's voice. "She's had you, hasn't she, Eli? How could she resist? How could you?"

"Now, Connie, you don't understand." Eli pleaded weakly. He had begun to cringe.

"Oh, but I do. You're a normal, healthy, big male animal—well, perhaps a bit bigger than normal. Anyway, nature would simply have had her way. You two would have developed an, ah, accommodation as a matter of course. In any case, I understand. Really I do."

"You do? Well, then, Connie, couldn't we—I mean, can't we just—"

"Kiss and make up?" Constance took on a droll tone. "Oh, I don't think so, Eli. Not now. Not here with her only a block or two away. Who would you spend the nights with? Which one of us would get the days?"

"There—there wouldn't be time for that. I—we— have to take the fort back from the mutineers. Somehow I have to get inside." Eli went on, planning aloud as he struggled to regain some of her esteem. "I have to find out what the situation is behind the walls. Then we can decide how to go about it."

"Won't that be dangerous?"

"No doubt. Without that knowledge, though, we're helpless. They have artillery, plenty of ammunition. Small arms and numbers against us, too. Even so, there is some weakness, and we have to find it out."

"Eli — I'll — be terribly worried about you while you're gone. Please, come back to me safely."

Constance kissed him then. Warmly, yet lacking the fervor of their earlier liaisons. Eli put his arms around her. Forgotten in the moment, his hat dropped to the floor. Eli's mighty member began to rise, and he considered if he had ample time to enjoy this bundle of delights once more before he made arrangements to sneak into Fort Rawlins. Their embrace ended, and he tried to renew it with greater warmth. Constance placed two fingers across his lips.

"Go now. If we keep this up, you may never be able to do your duty."

"How's that?"

Constance gave him a throaty chuckle. "Because you'll be too weak to climb the walls."

Out on the street once again, Eli encountered Lieutenant Strickland and a young man from the wagon train. They had, Thad explained, been looking for him.

"Lieutenant Strickland says that the insurrectionists in the fort must have cut the telegraph line," Gene Brent said after the introductions. "If so, maybe I can help. I've worked as a lineman and repairman. I have my own climbing gear. Even if they've cut out a section of wire, I can work around it somehow."

"That's a good idea, only I suspect they simply cut it

where it enters the fort. Or at the signal office itself. That would be simplest to do. I might be able to use some of your equipment, though. Do you have a pair of climbing spikes?"

"Yes. Two pair, as a matter of fact. I figured to get work with the telegraph company in Washington."

"Good. I'll need those. Now, if I can rig some sort of grapnel hook—"

"What do you plan to do, Eli?" Thad Strickland inquired.

"A young woman just told me how to go about it. Now I have the equipment I need. It's simple, Thad. We have to know what things are like inside Fort Rawlins, right? Well, I'm going to wait until late at night and climb the palisades to get a look."

Chapter 16

The drunken excesses of the men not directly involved with the looting of Fort Rawlins increased with
each day. Sometime during the early evening unknown
persons had set fire to one of the enlisted barracks. It
still glowed and pulsed as streams of dirty gray smoke
spiraled into the night sky. Eli Holten approached the
walls. Only a few alcohol-slurred voices came from
inside. The scout had pushed his Morgan stallion hard
so that he reached the vicinity of the fort two hours
before sundown.

At that time, the blaze leaped high into the air, and
excited shouting indicated the concern of at least some
of the mutinous soldiers that the entire post might go
up in flames. Holten made careful notes, based on his
observations through field glasses. His surveillance
lasted on into the night.

It gave him valuable information on the sentry
positions, or rather the lack of them. During the day,

only one man stood above the main gate. As darkness fell, two replaced that guard. A single, somewhat intoxicated soldier paced each of the four walls. Other than that, no provisions for security had apparently been taken. He considered entering the fort surreptitiously to be an easy matter.

Holten left Sonny in a draw a quarter mile from the fort. He had borrowed a uniform from one of Thad Strickland's troopers, which, though large, fitted his six-foot-two frame like rain-shrunken clothes. Tucked into the belt, he carried his Sioux moccasins. He had a twenty-foot length of stout rope around his middle, and one hand held a three-prong grapnel. Clutched in his left hand, he had the climbing spikes ready for use. Darkness, from an early setting moon, and booze became his allies as he crept up to the base of the wall.

The scout had chosen his place carefully. He would not attempt to go over the palisades near the front. Rather, he had selected to make his try along the rear of the large military installation, in the area of the stables. When he reached his desired position, he stopped and unwound the rope. One end he fastened to the grapnel and loosely coiled the rest. This he sat aside while he strapped the climbing spikes to his legs. Ready at last, he made a final check of the parapet before taking the grapnel line in hand.

At first he saw no sign of the sentry. Then, in the gloom, faintly illuminated by the glow of the dying fire, he saw his man at the far end of the platform, in deep conversation with the guard from the north side. If his luck held, Eli thought, he would have the grapnel set and be over the wall without either of them becoming suspicious. He hefted the coil of braided hemp and gave the dangling grapnel a hearty swing.

To Holten it sounded like the crack of doom when the metal points slammed into the back sides of the vertical logs that formed the palisades. Eli paused, hunkered low in the darker shadow of the wall for ten long, tense seconds. When no alarm came, he gave the rope a stout tug. One spade-shaped tip caught, held a second, then came free.

Disappointed, the scout pulled the device over the top, let it fall and rewound the line. A quick check to make sure it would travel cleanly and he tried again. Another loud clump. A moment later, a voice raised in query from the far corner.

"Who's there?"

"Take it easy, Granger."

"Didn' you hear that noise, Bob?"

"Sure. Happens all the time. Some drunk bastard fallin' on his ass. Don't let it get to you. Shit. We ain't on regular guard mount, you know."

"Yeah. But with them troopers ridin' up here yesterday an' all. You never know. They take this place back, our asses are fried."

"You want to check it out?"

"No," Granger answered. "What I really want to do is get the hell away from here. Run and keep on runnin' until someone sees this blue suit I got and says, 'What the hell are you wearin', stranger?' Now, *that's* what I surely do want."

"There's still a lot of Tangle-foot, Granger."

"Booze don't hold a candle to a noose. The guys who started this, anyone who sticks with 'em. Hell, the army's gonna hang the lot of 'em. I'd like to start out right now."

"How'd you get over the wall?"

"That's all's holdin' me back, Bob."

A short pause followed. Then Bob went on in a distant, speculative tone. "Truth to tell, Granger, I'd almost be willin' to come along with you."

"Let's do it, then. In the mornin', just before dawn. We can take a couple of horses, walk 'em out through the sally port and be away before anyone can be the wiser."

"Sounds — well, it sounds all right by me. You got a deal, Granger."

Holten waited an extra ten seconds after they stopped talking before he gave a heave on the line. The taut manila transmitted the bite as two points bit deeply into the pine. Eli leaned all his weight back on the rope and flushed with success as the grapnel held. He took two solid handholds on the rope and set his climbers into the soft wood of the palisade.

Slowly, hand over hand, his spike-fitted boots driving him upward, the scout squirmed his way up the outer face of the wall. When he reached the top, he paused below the line of sight and listened carefully until his ankles ached. Satisfied, he eased his head over the pointed poles and took a quick glance around. The sight he beheld froze him in place.

At one end of the parade ground, an odd-shaped scaffold squatted on the clean, white gravel. Two six-by-six uprights held in place a huge, ugly blade. Below it, Holten made out a long, slanting board that rested on a ledge along one side of the base. He also recognized a yoke, similar to those used on oxen, and a large wicker basket. A shudder passed through him, spawned by an old memory of something seen in a school book.

What in hell was one doing here at Fort Rawlins? The infernal device had but one function, Eli reminded himself. Sickened by the realization, he wondered if it had yet been used. And upon whom? The scout levered himself up with his powerful arms and swung a leg over the crenellations. The other quickly followed and he crouched low. Another, more familiar sight caught his attention.

At the far end of the parade, two huge wagon wheels, held erect by buried posts, indicated another form of punishment had been employed. Again, who had they been used on? From the sutler's store, two voices raised in drunken argument. The cause, like their words, were completely lost on the scout. Eli remained motionless, except for his eyes and swiveling head.

He quickly spotted two prone figures, inebriated soldiers who had fallen in mid-stride to lay curled in their own vomit while they snored in liquor-befuddled indifference. One had his head resting against the near end of the tie-rail in front of the headquarters building. A litter of broken bottles, torn paper, and human waste covered the once immaculate parade ground. Free spirit though he might be, this desecration wrinkled Eli's forehead in distaste. Confident that his arrival had gone undetected, he quickly removed his climbing gear and boots, stowed them in a dark recess, and put on his moccasins.

In stealthy silence, the scout worked his way along to the closest access ladder and lowered himself over the side of the parapet. He took the rungs cautiously, though swiftly, to prevent discovery. On the ground, he negotiated his way around the outer edges of the fort, from right to left. To his relief, he found no other guards. Tom Pierce had said that the officers and noncoms had been taken prisoner. The logical place for them would be the stockade. He made that his next place to investigate.

One man, dressed only in soiled uniform trousers and scuffed boots, sprawled across the OOD's desk. Thoroughly soused, as evidenced by the nearly empty whiskey bottle that lay on its side beside his face, he made fluttery popping sounds with his lips as he exhaled. Well beyond revival, by several glasses of liquor, he remained motionless as the scout entered and moved on cat feet to the heavy door that separated the guardroom from the cell block.

"Is General Corrington here?" Eli inquired in a harsh whisper.

"Eli? Is that you?" Frank Corrington's voice shook with suppressed emotion and weariness. He wanted to shout, to weep with relief and dance for joy. "I'm down here."

Holten quickly found him. His eyes narrowed at the sight of the general's condition. By the light of a single, dim candle lamp, the blistered, peeling skin and raw, ugly sores of the commanding officer's ordeal on the punishment wheel clearly showed. An angry growl lurked deep in Eli's throat as he examined his friend.

"Who is responsible for this?" Eli said by way of greeting.

"Howard Barryman. He's head of the mutiny. Him and an ex-trooper named Vince Liscomb."

"What was it done for?"

"We planned an escape, Eli. We were going to blow a

hole through the wall with gunpowder and break out. There was an informer, a young lieutenant named Brian Currey. I don't know his motives. Fear I suppose. Anyway, we got caught before we could give it a try. Barryman put Abner Styles and me out on the wagon wheels four days ago as punishment for the attempt."

"The major. How is he?"

Corrington's face crumpled into a visage of concern. "Not so good, I'm afraid. He's been unconscious since the middle of the afternoon. Not even water or coffee could revive him. He feels hot as a fireplace poker. How soon can you get us out of here?"

"It will take a while. After they opened up with those gallopers yesterday, Thad Strickland withdrew the troops and that civilian wagon train to Eagle Pass. I have to gather what information I can and return there before we can make another attack on the fort."

Frank Corrington frowned. "Hummm. That will never do."

"Why's that, sir?"

"Abner and I are scheduled to have our heads cut off on that damned guillotine at sunset, day after tomorrow."

The general's words chilled Eli Holten. "That doesn't leave much time, does it."

"A forced march both ways, I'm afraid, Eli."

"We can handle that. It would save some time if I could send someone back to Thad right away."

"That might be possible, Eli. Not all of the men are behind this mutiny. Some are going along, making the motions to prevent being murdered. Barryman is insane and his partner in crime, Vince Liscomb, is even worse."

"What about this Lieutenant Currey?"

"He came back here for a while. Not for long, though. Two of our more junior lieutenants beat the living hell out of him. At last he had to go over entirely to the mutineers. He's one of them now."

"That's idiotic. There's no way they can win. What does Currey expect to gain?"

"Who knows? All I know is that I wish I had been strong enough and gotten *my* hands on him."

Holten reflected on it a moment. "I can take care of that little matter later on. For now, I want to get more of a look at the fort. Any idea who I might contact about giving us help?"

"There was a trooper—I don't remember his name now—who was guarding us. He said he wanted to end all this, give control back to the officers. He and some of the others, I gathered. Or you can talk with some of the NCOs. Those who aren't here are locked up in one of the buildings."

"That sounds like a start. And don't worry about your turncoat, Currey, Frank. I'll take care of that before this is over."

A few minutes after midnight, Patty Cramer slipped up to the windowless shed at the blacksmithy that had been commandeered to house one prisoner, Frank Reamer. The others had barely fitted in the small new Eagle Pass jail. She sighed in relief when she saw no sign of a guard, while her heart pounded in excitement. It didn't matter what they said about him.

Frankie was not like that. He was good and kind and loving. Oh, so loving. Why, he had twice as much pecker as any of those silly little boys she had fooled around with before. She just couldn't *stand* to be away from Frankie for long. Pulse throbbing, nipples stiff with erotic readiness, she hurried to the door and fumbled with a heavy, stubborn slide bolt.

"Wha—what is it?" Frank Reamer groaned as he came out of a deep sleep to find eager fingers probing at his fly.

"It's—me—Patty. Oh, Frankie, I couldn't stand it any longer. I had to come to you."

"My God! Patty—you—you could get in a lot of trouble." This could turn out to be quite an advantage, Reamer's crafty mind exalted. "Here, let me help you."

Quickly Frank undid his fly and held it open while Patty plunged inside and withdrew his flaccid organ. She squeezed and petted it in a frenzy, oblivious to their surroundings.

"Oooh, poor thing. He's all limp and wrinkled. Patty knows what to do. I'll straighten him out quick enough." She bent low and took the warm flesh deep into her soft, moist, willing mouth.

Somehow this horny little girl could be used to help him escape. Reamer felt sure of that. What would he do once he and the other boys got free? Not much choice. Might as well throw in with those soldiers who rebelled. They had a lot of weapons, and surely they would be planning to get away from the fort soon. Safety in their numbers, that was for sure. Despite all his distracted calculations, Frank's penis swelled to fullness under the exquisite manipulations of Patty's lips and tongue.

Slurping joyfully, Patty murmured her appreciation of Frank's rapid response and sought to take more into her pulsating throat. With her tongue she diligently teased the silken flesh. Frank began to tremble and quickly realized that he had better come up with some ideas quickly and get an agreement from Patty. Before too much of this went on and he forgot about it entirely.

"Ah, Patty. Remember when you helped me before? When you got our guns for us?"

"Mummph-ummph."

"Well, you can help me a whole lot again."

"Murrrmff?"

"I have to get out of here. I have to escape. Being cooped up is awful, and it will make me sick." Reamer thought of the inevitable noose that awaited him for the murder charge. "Can you do it? You got in here easy enough. Can you let me out so I can get away from here?"

With a loud, liquid plop, Patty removed her suctioning mouth and stared blank-eyed up at Frank. "I—don't know, Frankie. It might mean a lot of trouble for me. Would you take me along so I don't get in trouble for it?"

"I, uh, imagine that could be arranged."

"Oh, goodie!" Her dress rustled as she hiked it up around her waist and yanked down on her bloomers. "Now hurry. Put it in me, Frankie. Put it deep, deep inside and churn around and around. I like it when you do that. It makes me feel so-o-o-o good."

"I have an idea."

"What's that?"

"It'll make you feel better than ever before. I'll do it for you if you promise to help me an' the boys get away from here."

197

"All—right—Frankie. I'll do it. Only you gotta take me along. Now, what's this new way to have fun?"

"Stand up and spread your legs wide. That's it. That's a good girl. Now, bend far over."

"You gonna put it in my behind?"

"No, Patty. I'm gonna stick it in your front end from in back. It'll give you a real thrill."

"Oooh. Hurry, hurry. I'm gettin' all juicy waitin'."

"Promise? Promise to help me tomorrow night."

"Y-e-s-s, Frankie. If we—if we can do this forever."

"Count on it. I even know how we can do it in the saddle when we ride away from Eagle Pass tomorrow night." *And it'll be the last time to have to put up with you,* Yellowstone Frank Reamer thought coldly as he inserted his bulging phallus into her steamy trough.

Chapter 17

Eli Holten pressed his face close to the rough wood of a small supply annex next to the quartermaster warehouse. He had asked his question through a crack between siding boards in a harsh whisper and waited tensely for the answer.

"Until someone gets us out of here, there ain't a hell of a lot we can do, Mr. Holten," Sergeant Hirt prefaced his response. "There's two fellers I know of who don't like this mutiny any more than we do. At least they're on the outside. Trooper Randisi and Trooper Sirak. You could see what they might do."

"Fine. All I have to do is locate them in this madhouse."

"Shouldn't be too hard," Douglas Hirt suggested. "They spend most of their time in Lieutenant Strickland's hutment on officers' row. You can find them there, I'm sure. They try to keep out of the way of Barryman and his rotten crew. They aren't like the rest of those yardbirds. Don't get mixed up in the drinkin' and hell raisin'. Sirak has helped us out a bit from time to time. Slipped us some blankets and extra food."

"Good. I'll see what I can set up with them."

Like a wraith, the scout slipped from shadow to shadow to the wide company street that gave access to officers' row. He took a deep breath, a quick glance to right and left and crossed the open space. His moccasin-clad feet made no sound on the hard-packed dirt. Once more he started darting from spot to spot until he reached the quarters assigned to his friend. A light rap on the door brought a prompt response.

"Who is it?"

"Holten."

"What the hell?" Trooper Randisi blurted. "Is this some sort of trick?"

"No. Let me in. I need to talk to you two."

An urgent, whispered conversation went on inside. Then another voice spoke. "How do we know it really is Eli Holten?"

Holten recognized the slight accent. "It's Joe Sirak who asked me that. You're from Florida and you like to play three-card Monte. I took two months' pay from you in a game last December."

"Damn. I never told anyone about that. Open the door, Bob."

Randisi slid the wooden bolt and swung the portal open a narrow crack. Still cautious, he peered out a second before he stepped back and let Eli in.

"How did you get here?" he inquired of the scout.

"Over the wall. What I need right now is some help. Sergeant Hirt told me you two had nothing to do with the mutiny. I want one of you to volunteer to get a horse out of here and ride to Eagle Pass. Lieutenant Strickland is there with five troopers and Corporal Boyle. Tell him to get started at once and I'll meet the column on the trail sometime around mid-morning."

"What good can seven men do?" Joe Sirak inquired.

"Thad has around a dozen civilian volunteers from a wagon train and twenty Sioux warriors with him. By the time we link up, I'll have a good idea on the situation here, and we can work out a plan of attack."

"Twenty Sioux braves?" Randisi asked in a wondering tone. He reached up to idly scratch his thick, black hair and shook his head in disbelief. "I know they fought against that Limey at Breakneck Gap, but how did the lieutenant manage to get 'em to take a side in this?"

Eli gave the troopers a rueful smile. "He didn't. They invited themselves along. You can find out about it when you reach Eagle Pass. Now, who's up for a long ride?"

"I'll go," Joe Sirak offered.

"I will," Randisi added.

"Why don't you both head out. That way it insures the chances of my message getting through. Muffle your horses' hoofs and lead them away from the fort for a good ways before mounting up. I'll see about stirring up something in here to keep the attention off of you."

"Thanks, Mr. Holten," Bob Randisi said sincerely.

"What do you figure to do?" Joe Sirak inquired.

"I don't know. Something noisy and probably dangerous enough that no one will be gazing out over the prairie. There's been one fire. It could happen again."

"That's destroying government property," Sirak protested. A quartermaster clerk, he handled the accounting figures for expenditures and losses at the fort. It made him inordinately money conscious.

Holten flashed a white grin. "Somehow, if I manage to

get this mutiny broken up as a result, I don't think anyone is going to send me a bill for anything I destroy. Now, get to it. And—be careful."

Patty Cramer's silky naked body pressed against Frank Reamer's hairy chest as she sat straddled in his lap. She locked her ankles behind his back and violently undulated her pelvis to drive his stiff organ deep inside her hot, most cleft.

"Unnnh—aaaaah—n-now—n-n-n-now—oooooh—a-a-a-ah!" She panted as she worked her way to a magnificent, tingly climax.

The small girl panted and grunted, eyes rolling wildly as she continued to impale herself on his turgid phallus. She groaned and ground herself harder as she felt him swelling inside her and sensed his moment rapidly approaching. Patty bent forward and began to lick and nip at his rigid nipples, slathering her tongue over his muscular torso in wild abandon while her jangling nerves signaled her own spiraling rise to yet another burst of splendor. Skillfully she tightened the muscles around her burning passage and trembled at Frank's gush of release.

Shaken to the core, she remained in position, his throbbing lance buried to the hilt, while they slowly came down from the pinnacle. Patty placed her cheek against his and spoke softly once reason returned.

"It's all set up, Frankie. I stole the keys to the jail. When we get done here, we'll go free with your friends and ride away into the night."

"You're a good girl, Patty."

Her shivery response tightly clasped his member which was still rigid.

"You are also the best lover I've ever known," Frank lied.

"Really?" Patty exclaimed in childish delight. "Am I the youngest?"

"Uh—well, no. There was one I knew a long time ago. She was only eleven. Of course, I was just fourteen myself."

"Oh, my! You started early." She paused a moment, then added impishly, "Like me."

Reamer stirred and reached for his shirt. "We had better go."

"Oh, can't we—just one more time?"

Her plea came with a squeezing, sliding invitation he could not refuse.

Slowly at first, then with increasing vigor, Patty began to drive her pelvis forward and back, slamming the swollen mound of her pubic arch against the sensitive skin above his wet, reddened penis. Anxious to be away from Eagle Pass, the army, and captivity, Frank hoped to finish this quickly, though he couldn't help enjoying it to the limit.

What a talented little thing Patty was. Too bad they had to end it on this night, Frank lamented, as he strove to match her rhythm, and he drove himself even deeper into her crevice. A moan of pleasure rose from deep in his chest, and he bent to take one of her tiny breasts into his eager mouth.

Howard Barryman awakened groggily in the big bed in Frank Corrington's quarters. He glanced around and then settled a scowl on Myron Henshaw. "What the hell are you doing here? It's still dark outside."

"I just received word from my other agent. Eli Holten is on his way here to try getting inside the fort."

"So what? What can one man do? That's not worth

waking me in the middle of the night. Now, go on and let me sleep."

"Howard, you wanted a piece of the action in Baja Californa. If you expect to keep it, you had better start thinking clearer than that. Holten could be here right this minute. What if he let the officers go and armed them? And the noncoms you've got in that storage shed? Everyone's drunk around here, except you and me. They could take this place back in ten minutes. You'd better find someone sober enough and turn out a larger guard force than you have. Men who'll stay awake."

"You're worried over nothing, I tell you," Barryman protested.

"Like hell I am! I opened the gate and walked in here and *not a single sentry challenged me*. What are you running around here?"

"It sure isn't a spit-and-polish army post, Henshaw," Barryman snarled. He had a headache and his stomach burned with greasy fire. Maybe they shouldn't have locked up the cooks. "How did you find this out anyway?"

"My agent in Eagle Pass came directly to our camp. Holten's put it about that he's going to find some weakness and then work out a way to attack this place and take it back. If you and these idiots are no more alert than right now, he just might do it, too."

"We have the cannon," Howard reminded him.

"And no one in condition to use them. Damnit, I don't intend to be caught in the middle of this. Ordinarily, it would be against my judgment to do this, but I'm going to move my men and the teamsters inside the fort to reinforce you. I wouldn't have put someone in place far in advance if I didn't know Holten was a handful for anyone. He has to be watched, taken out of the game if possible.

204

"It's too late for that now," Henshaw went on in exasperation. "But that's no excuse for this slovenly lash-up you have here. With Holten on the loose, you have to be doubly cautious. I'll be back here within two hours with the boys."

"How about this secret operative of yours? Will he be coming along?"

"There's no other option at this time. Watch for us. And this time I expect to be challenged before I get within fifty yards of the gate."

Barryman realized the sense of what Henshaw proposed. In light of the fact Eli Holten was in the area, it wouldn't hurt to double the guard. "You can be sure of that, Myron. I'll get someone on it at once."

Under normal circumstances, a burning outhouse might not generate a great deal of excitement. When it had been designed to accommodate fifteen troopers at a time, Eli Holten supposed, it might create an atmosphere of near pandemonium. It would, he felt certain, at least serve his dual purpose.

While the loyal troopers, Randisi and Sirak, made good their escape during this diversion, Eli figured to get back to the parapet, rig his climbing gear and disappear over the wall. A tidy bit of strategy and none too soon. He had heard the noisy arrival of a rider some ten minutes ago and the equally speedy departure. Whatever the purpose, it couldn't help him any. He sighed in resignation and glanced at the pile of debris on the floor.

The scout bent low over the small mound of paper and slivers of wood. He scratched a lucifer match on the polished board seat of a toilet hole and touched the flame to his kindling. An irregular, crimson and yellow circle spread out from that point, leaving a pit of blackness behind. Rapidly the blaze grew. Time to leave.

Outside, the scout sprinted to the protective blackness at the base of the wall. Immediately he noticed that the sentries had been increased in number and were considerably more alert. Cautiously, he began to work his way around to the ladder near where he had left his climbing spikes and grapnel. Although all around him the mutinous occupants of Fort Rawlins slept, getting out, he surmised, would not be easy. Suddenly, from almost directly above him, a voice called out. "Fire! Fire! Everybody wake up. There's a shithouse on fire!"

Eli froze while men began to stir and sit up. They yelled, then began to stagger drunkenly out of barracks and run toward the burning building. Others joined them, some from where they had lain in stuporous slumber along the walls or in the stable. In this milling confusion, Eli stepped into the open and trotted purposefully toward the ladder he sought.

To his surprise and relief, no one interrupted him, and he made it to the outer wall unmolested. He put one foot on a rung and climbed rapidly. As his head cleared the platform, he saw another sentry's back not fifteen feet from him. He stealthily raised himself higher while one hand stole to his belt, and he closed fingers over the haft of his big bowie knife.

With a lunge, Eli came over the lip of the parapet and sprang upright. His swift movement alerted the guard, who turned around hurriedly, irritated that someone had snuck up on him as a prank.

"Who the hell—" He broke off and swallowed heavily when he recognized the person in front of him. "Oh, fuck—*Mr. Holten!*"

In wild desperation, the sentry swung his rifle like a club, hands wrapped around the barrel near the muzzle. Eli ducked under the uncoordinated attack, and starlight reflected in silver pools off the wide blade of his bowie as he drew it and thrust forward.

Cold steel entered vulnerable flesh in the trooper's belly. It sliced through muscle and the peritoneum with fiery ease and entered his bowels. With a violent twist of his powerful wrist, the scout turned the blade and ripped upward.

The hapless mutineer opened his mouth roundly in a soundless scream as the keen edge sliced through his intestines, liver, and stomach, spilling the contents of the latter into the bloody soup of his abdominal cavity. He dropped the rifle and staggered backward two steps. With the swiftness of an eyeblink, he fell away from the lip of the platform onto the ground below. His departure pulled the knife free and Eli held it, his hand and forearm drenched with blood, which dripped, along with a steady stream from the tip of his bowie, onto the boards that formed the parapet. After only a moment's span to wipe his weapon clean, the scout ducked low and duck-walked to where he had left his equipment.

Fortunately the new guard had not located it. Holten strapped on the spikes and set his grapnel in the soft pine of two poles that formed the palisade. He took the loose rope in his hands and swung a leg over the pointed tops of the wall. When the climber sank into resinous wood, he followed with the other foot and began a rapid descent.

Once on the ground, the scout shook his grapnel free, coiled the manila line and hurried off into the night. Behind him the sounds of confusion and excitement grew.

"Now that we're away from town, Frankie, when are we going to do it again?" Patty asked as she rubbed her excited and tingling crotch.

"Right now, if you want," Yellowstone Frank Reamer told her. "You boys ride on ahead. Patty an' me have something to, ah, take care of."

"Sure, Frank," came a snickering reply.

By the time his men had ridden beyond sight, Frank and Patty had dismounted from his horse. She came into his open arms and hugged close to his big chest. Frank heard her rough, sensual breathing and tasted the sweetness of her breath.

"I itch somethin' awful, Frankie. Runnin' away like this got me all hot and bothered. Hurry, get your clothes off. Then you can do some special things to thank me for helping you."

"Oh, I intend to, Patty. Pull your dress up, like a good girl."

Patty Cramer reached down and grasped the hem of her plain cotton print dress and hauled it up over her slender body until its frilly edges covered her face. She didn't hear the four clicks as Frank Reamer cocked his Colt revolver.

The bullet entered the back of Patty's head and bulged her eyes before it exited through her mouth in a shower of blood, brain tissue, and teeth chips.

She died still loving Frank and the wonderful things he did to her.

Chapter 18

A thick curtain of silence fell on the plains. One moment the meadowlarks warbled, quail cheekily whistled, and insects buzzed endlessly. The next, no sound reached the scout's ears. Not even the steady drumming of his Morgan's hoofs penetrated the quietude. It was as though he had been deprived of his hearing. The late afternoon sun slanted down toward the horizon, and Eli Holten realized he had been without sleep for more than forty-eight hours.

The human machine can endure only so much before the senses tire and begin to shut down of their own accord. Such a condition assailed Holten as he rode toward his anticipated rendezvous with Lieutenant Strickland and the make-do force the officer commanded. Somehow, before the attack on the fort, he would have to get some sleep. His eyes felt gritty and dry, the lids heavy. He perked up only slightly when he detected movement far to the west and, a minute later, saw a rising column of wispy brown dust. Fifteen minutes, perhaps. Holten guided Sonny toward the approaching column and urged greater speed. Although he sat upright and outwardly alert, the scout slowly slipped off into a fitful doze.

"Mr. Holten coming in, sir," Corporal Boyle called to Lieutenant Strickland.

"I see him, corporal. If I didn't know better, I'd say he was sound asleep in the saddle."

"That he is, sir, or I'm an Englishman born," the Dublin-born NCO responded in an amused tone. "He'll be more'n one night shy of rest. By your leave, sir, an' I'll ride out to him."

"Go ahead, Boyle."

Holten seemed awake enough when he pulled Sonny to a halt beside his friend. "Howdy, Thad. I've had a good look and with a little luck, we should be able to take the fort back with a minimum of losses."

"How many are we facing?"

"Those who will actually fight — maybe twenty. They have those two gallopers on the wall over the main gate. The only real artillerymen on the post aren't cooperating. I sent two of them to you, which leaves only Sergeant Goreman, who's locked up, and a pair of loaders who won't help Barryman's mutineers. So their accuracy is knocked in a buffalo wallow."

"Along with any speed in loading. I noticed that the other day. Your two messengers insisted on coming with us, as you can see. How do you figure to do this?"

"I've been thinking it over, Thad. Remember when Broken Bow attacked the wagon train? They came at one angle only. Not the usual fighting style, but it did concentrate all the defenders' attention to one side of the circle. Now the fort's like a defensive ring of wagons in a way. Those cannon can only shoot one direction at a time."

"I see what you're leading up to," Strickland interrupted. "And I think it might work. Only are you going to suggest we put all our troops into that attack?"

"No. I have something else in mind." Holten frowned and changed the subject. "When Boyle came out to meet me, he mentioned that Reamer and his men escaped."

"Yes, damnit. It seems that the Cramer girl, Patty, had a hot romance going with Reamer."

"She's just a child!" the scout exploded.

"*Was* just a child," Thad told him. "From the looks of what has happened, I think we can assume that Patty was responsible for Reamer and his men getting their weapons back before the Sioux showed up. Anyway, she broke him out of the storage shed where we'd locked him up. He freed his men, they armed themselves and rode out of Eagle Pass last night. Took Patty along." Anger and regret at what he saw as a personal failure colored Strickland's face a dark crimson.

"Then, to show his gratitude for all her help, Reamer killed the girl. Shot her in the back of the head. When we discovered them missing, Gray Beaver and two other Sioux offered to track Reamer's crew. They found the girl's body and reported it, then went on. I expect them when we stop for the night."

"We can't be stopping too long. It's another twenty miles to Fort Rawlins. We have to be in position to attack at dawn. It won't be too hard for Gray Beaver to find us, even it we move on."

"All right, then. We can halt for a meal, rest the

horses, then push on."

"Good. I laid out some contingency plans with the captive officers and noncoms. They're locked up but if we get inside the fort, we can have them out in no time."

"You're going inside again?"

"No. *We* are. While the attack is made on one side of the fort, you and the troops you have with you are going through the water gate and stable yard so we can hit them in the rear. I'll go over the wall to let you in."

"Do you like doing things the hard way or are you just a sucker for danger?"

"Have a better idea, Thad?"

Strickland scowled. "No. Can't say that I do. We'll keep moving until dusk. Which should put us within striking distance of the fort. That way the men and horses can get maximum rest."

"Sounds good to me. I could use a few hours' sleep."

"That's for sure. You look like a risen corpse. Well, time to eat miles. For-ward, at the trot," the young officer commanded, "ma-a-rch!"

Fatback sizzled and popped in skillets, and a big pot of beans bubbled over a fire for the white troops and their civilian volunteers by the time Gray Beaver returned to the column. The Sioux had their own campfire, where a small antelope roasted over a bed of coals that licked up spurts of flame as juices dropped onto it. The Quill Worker chief avoided its welcoming aroma in order to report to Lieutenant Strickland.

"Tall Bear is with us, I see," the Sioux said cheerfully. "Now we can take care of the bad whites with ease. Stri'k-lan'," he addressed himself to the lieutenant. "The bad men are not far from here. They go toward the soldier lodge called Rawlins."

"I wonder why? I would think that would be the last place they would want to head, knowing we plan to attack."

"Not really," Eli contradicted. "They know our plans, not the details, but enough to buy them protection. And perhaps swing the balance toward the mutineers. Reamer's basically a coward. Being caught alone on the prairie by a force our size would not be his idea of a good choice."

"We eat first, then go back," Gray Beaver declared. "Take Tall Bear, two men and kill Reamer, then we sleep well until fight at soldier lodge."

Holten started to rise. "Sounds like a good idea to me."

Yellowstone Frank Reamer stumbled over a rock. "Goddamnit!"

"What's the matter, cap?" Drake Ferrel inquired.

"Rock. Damned near busted my toe. I hate ridin' at night. Hate walkin' even more."

"The horses are tired, cap," Pete Leach spoke up. "You said so yourself."

"You pushin' me, boy?" A dangerous note sounded in Reamer's voice.

"Leave the kid alone," Pete's brother, Hank, grumbled. "He's only talkin' to hear himself."

"We've come too far together to start pickin' at each other," Issac Kilgore offered. "We'd best push on to that fort."

"Y'er right, Ike," Reamer responded, somewhat subdued. "Mount up, boys, and we'll make tracks."

Issac Kilgore screamed for reply. He tottered a

213

moment against the frosty white background of stars, then fell from his saddle with an arrow between his shoulder blades.

"What the fuck!" Pete Leach blurted out.

"Down!" Frank Reamer shouted.

Hunkered in the tall grass, Reamer and his surviving men took advantage of the skyline to search for their unknown attackers. A long half a minute went by without a sound, other than the nervous snorting of their mounts, disturbed by the smell of blood. Another thirty seconds crept by. Still no sign of whoever had killed Issac. A sudden, brief rustle in the tall stalks sent Reamer spinning around.

He fired hastily at a dark form that flitted across the star pattern and missed. A moment later a gurgling wail rose from where he had seen Pete Leach dive into hiding.

"Pete!" Hank Leach screamed. "Petey! Are you hurt? Answer me."

"Get down!" Reamer growled at him.

Too late. Hank rose to a crouch and rushed toward where he had last seen his brother.

"God! Oh, God, no!" the young hardcase wailed. "Petey—oh, Petey!"

At his feet lay his brother, grinning at him from a wetly new, gaping set of lips an inch below his jaw. A spreading pool of blood inched outward and touched the toe of Hank's boot. Half a second later, Frank heard the eerie, whirring moan of an arrow in flight.

Hank Leach stiffened and came upright. The feathered butt of a Sioux arrow protruded from his chest. He gagged and staggered, while his right lung filled with crimson liquid. Another shaft whistled on its way to put him out of his misery. The point struck a rib and deflected slightly, so that the pounded metal tip sliced through the bottom lobe of his heart. It continued onward, pushing through the muscle tissue on the left side of his spine and protruded through his back, dripping gore. Leach sank into the buffalo grass with a soft groan.

"The bastards are all around us!" Drake Ferrel screamed as he began to pump bullets wildly into the darkness, his night vision destroyed by the yellow-orange muzzle bloom.

"Move, get away from there and reload," Frank Reamer called out to him.

He quickly followed his own advice, wondering at how calm he remained. Usually he left the heroics to others. He saw a figure outlined against the pattern of stars and fired at nearly point-blank range. A sharp cry and the thud of a body hitting the ground told him he had found his mark. He heard movement off to his left and whirled that way.

Frank saw nothing but the silhouettes of grass stalks waving in the light breeze. He heard, though, when Drake Ferrel squealed like a pig and his feet thrashed the ground.

Gutted, Frank thought, sickened by the image it conjured up. A new chill gripped at his heart. That meant he was alone out here with many Sioux warriors. Frank stiffened when he heard a rustle in the sedge to his right. He whirled on one boot heel.

Standing only a few feet from his hiding place, he recognized the tall, wide-shouldered frame of Eli Holten. Instead of the usual Winchester, the scout held a short, powerful Indian bow. He had an arrow nocked and pulled back for release.

For a moment, neither man moved. Then Frank Reamer eased up the muzzle of his six-gun until it covered the center of Holten's chest. In the same instant, Eli let go the buffalo gut string.

His fletched messenger of death sped true to the target.

Reamer's bullet went wide.

The sharpened steel point bit into flesh an inch above Reamer's abdomen, and his slight paunch absorbed the shaft until only the turkey-feathered butt protruded. Behind him, the arrow pinned Frank to the ground.

Agony beyond comprehension exploded in Frank Reamer's stomach. He wanted to howl like a dog at the moon, but he only writhed feebly. He dropped the Colt and carefully placed both hands around the shaft that held him in place. His mouth worked for a second before any sound came.

"Holten — you — bastard. How many savages did you bring along?"

"Only three and you killed one of those. I suppose I should turn you over to them to play with rather than finishing you off myself."

"No! Please. Anything but that. Have mercy and finish me yourself." Images of Sioux torture rose to haunt him.

"Like you did for the Cramer girl?"

"You, uh, know about that, eh?"

"Why'd you do it, Reamer? She'd done nothing to harm you."

"I — it was an accident, honest it was."

"Shot in the back of the head? *Why*, Reamer?"

"She was a lousy fuck," Reamer responded flippantly, despite the incredible agony deep in his gut.

Then, as though unable to die with such a statement on his conscience, he made a depreciating gesture in an attempt to wave away the words. "That's not it at all. She was good. One of the best I've ever had. Only she was so—so stupid. Cowlike and hot to do it all the time. Maybe that's why. I just couldn't face that for months on end."

Holten took another step closer. As he did, he released the tension on his bow and clutched it and another arrow in his left hand. He glared down at Reamer, filled with loathing and disgust.

"That still leaves you near the top of the list of rotten sons of bitches."

"Y-you ain't gonna kill me in cold blood, are you Holten?" As he spoke in a whining voice, Frank Reamer reached steathily toward his abandoned revolver. His cold fingers closed over the thick barrel, and he worked it into position to grip.

"Not in cold blood at all, Reamer. I think I'll enjoy watching them stretch your neck."

"No you won't!" Reamer yelled in triumph as his finger closed around the trigger of his Colt.

Flame lanced from the muzzle, and made a bullet sped toward the empty sky. Eli Holten no longer stood where he had. He caught the blur of motion as Reamer hurried his weapon into place. As he did, Eli's hand slid the wooden-handled, steel-head tomahawk from the belt that girded his lean, hard stomach and raised it high in an overhead position.

The air whistled as it descended.

Yellowstone Frank Reamer's head made a sound like

a split melon when the keen edge slid through his skull and a ruin of his brain. Blood, fluid, and mangled tissue bubbled around the smooth faces of the tomahawk for a second before Eli wrenched it free.

"The others are all dead," Gray Beaver told the scout as he walked up to where Holten stood over Reamer's convulsing body.

"Good. We had better be getting back to the column."

"First we take hair."

"Do whatever you want," Holten responded flatly. He felt drained, somehow dirtied by contact with Frank Reamer. Holten didn't regret the cowardly wagon master's death at his hands, only the uselessness of it all. Under other, better, circumstances, Reamer could have been an asset. Worse still, the fort remained to be dealt with.

Eli Holten slipped quietly away from the detachment of civilian volunteers and Strickland's troopers, who waited two hundred yards from Fort Rawlins. The heavy blackness that follows false dawn blanketed the prairie, and the scout had no doubt that he would be able to enter the fort easier than the first time.

He worked his way through the low-cropped grass to a spot opposite the wall furthest from any activity. He had allowed himself fifteen minutes to complete the task he set himself and be at the water gate by the creek that ran past the stable yard. Strickland and Pierce would be there then with the men who would enter the post and attack the mutineers from the rear. He climbed with ease and waited a long count of twenty before easing his way over the parapet and down onto the ground.

Quietly Holten detoured around the parade ground,

218

once more giving a baleful glance at the guillotine. When he reached officers' row, he paused a second, then darted from shadow to shadow until he located the quarters assigned to Lieutenant Currey.

"Don't make a sound or any attempt to struggle," the scout whispered huskily as he held his hand tightly over the traitorous lieutenant's mouth.

"Murrrmph?"

"It's Eli Holten. I made a promise to General Corrington to take care of you. I thought I had better get it over with before the fighting starts and you get forgotten in the confusion."

Currey tensed himself on his bunk and strained against Holten's hand.

"Don't move, I said. What do you think you accomplished by betraying your fellow officers? Do you suppose it made things easier for you? Well, I'll tell you what you bought. You're going to die, Currey. Right here and right now."

Although filled with terror, Brian Currey arched his back violently and heaved with all his strength. So intense was his effort to escape, so powerful the horror that welled within him at the prospect of his death, that he didn't feel the fire-and-ice pain as Holten's bowie slit a shallow line around his neck.

Blood ran freely down Currey's naked chest as he grabbed frantically for his holstered revolver. His fingers fumbled with the clasp as Eli Holten came at him again. In sheer desperation, Currey swung the entire pistol belt as the scout closed in on him.

The heavy holster struck Holten's knife hand, and the bowie went flying. It made a solid clunk when it hit the floor. Currey scrambled backward then and reached upward for his sabre, hung beside the bed. Holten plowed into Currey's middle and drove him to the far end of the mattress. Then he sent a looping punch to the left side of Currey's head.

Dazed, eyes glassy, Currey snapped backward, but not before he delivered a powerful kick square in the scout's crotch. The air whooshed out of Holten's mouth, and a rising gorge of sickness threatened him.

Weakened and reeling, Eli fell from the bed, both hands clutching his aching testicles as he curled into a protective ball. Currey snatched at his holster again and managed to free the big .45 Colt. Fear and despair blazing from his eyes, he peered over the edge at the groaning scout.

Before he could bring up the muzzle or cock the hammer, Holten recovered with a solid punch to the turncoat lieutenant's mouth. Teeth splintered and Currey flew backward. Tears ran down his face, and he spit out a mouthful of blood and broken ivory. To his instant horror, he realized he had dropped his revolver. Eli Holten rose from the floor and came at him again.

Once more, Brian Currey retreated to where he kept his sabre. This time, Holten beat him to it. Currey winced and began to whimper at the raspy metallic sound of the long, curved blade being drawn from its scabbard.

Then the scout had it against Currey's bare chest. The point bit in slightly, and the cowardly traitor tried a second time to kick Holten in the groin.

He succeeded, a split second after Holten slammed the sabre home, driving the point through Brian Currey's heart and left lung. The false edge grated on a rib as the long faces of the blade slid through tissue and poked out the back. Eli's superior strength forced it on until the tip split the mattress and buried itself in a wooden slat. Then the scout bent his arm sharply sideways and snapped the blade in two. A fitting end, he felt, as he slumped onto the floor.

It could have been hours, though actually only ten minutes, that Eli Holten lay on the floor while Currey's blood dripped methodically down into a pool from the bed above. Slowly the agony left him. At last he could stand without doubling over and walk with only slight discomfort.

He felt as though his whole body had been boiled in oil. Limping slightly, dragging one leg, the scout left the gory scene in Currey's quarters and started to the end of officers' row. There he turned and made his way slowly around the outside of the parade ground to the entrance of the stable yard.

With each step, his energy revitalized and the misery abated slightly. He crossed behind the hay scale and along the side of the ricks of firewood stored in the yard, until he reached the sally port that opened onto the watering station at the creek.

On the other side, Thad Strickland waited anxiously. He extended an eager hand and shook with Eli when the portal swung open. "I began to think you'd been found out. What have you been doing?"

"Trying to get my nuts kicked off. I had to finish off Currey. Promised the general I'd tend to it. He almost finished me instead. Come on inside. We'll free the officers first, then the NCOs in the warehouse. Then all we have to do is wait for Gray Beaver."

Chapter 19

Two men snored in the bunks of the guardroom. Whiskey bottles littered the floor, along with crushed cigar butts and wads of paper. Swift work with knifes, on the part of Lieutenant Strickland's troopers, ended the mutineers' lives. It took only seconds to open the heavy, iron-bound door to the cell block. Quickly the soldiers went along the corridor, urging quiet and opening barred doors. The officers and lead NCOs of Fort Rawlins stepped out into freedom. Faces lit up with joy; they eagerly accepted the weapons pressed into their hands.

"By God, it's good to see you Eli," General Corrington gusted out. "I — I'd almost given up hope. Have you taken the rest of the fort as yet?"

"No, sir. We'll need all the shooters we can field to do that. Our next stop is the quartermaster warehouse, to free the other noncoms."

"Sir, Lieutenant Strickland, sir. I — suppose the command is yours again, sir."

"No. No, Strickland. I'm not feeling all that well. You and Eli have figured this whole thing out, so go ahead and run the show." Twinkling eyes betrayed his pleasure in granting this favor.

"Why, thank you, sir. I would be honored. Uh — a suggestion, sir. While we free the rest of the NCOs, it would be better for you to wait in here. When the shooting starts outside, then you can come out, form into squads and pick your targets. They'll probably all be on the north wall, or close to it."

"How are you going to manage that? And what shooting from outside, lieutenant?"

"Uh — we've arranged a little diversion, sir. It should take all of the attention off the inside of the fort."

"But, damnit, mister, what sort of diversion?"

"The, ah, Sioux are going to attack the fort, sir."

General Corrington stared blankly at Thad Strickland for a long moment and shook his head. "Uh, yes, of course. The Sioux are on hand for this, I presume?"

"Yes, sir. They helped us escort the wagon train to here, then on to Eagle Pass."

"Certainly. Of course. The Sioux always help us escort wagon trains. How very thoughtful of them. Tell me, lieutenant, has captivity addled my brain or are we actually having this conversation?"

"Oh, it's real enough, sir."

"Yes. Well, ah, yes. Sort of like your little escapade against Weatherby over in the Black Hills, eh, Eli?"

"Much the same, sir," Holten admitted straight-faced.

"Good. Good. All right, then, lieutenant, get on with it."

"Yes, sir."

A pale ribbon of pink stretched along the eastern horizon by the time the quartermaster warehouse annex had been entered and the prisoners liberated. Eager for a fight, the sergeants and corporals fondled their Springfield carbines and repeatedly checked their ammunition supply. They crowded anxiously near the door and waited for a signal to attack the rebels within the walls. The thunder of many galloping hoofs came from beyond the fort. It brought smiles of rapture to the faces of the recently confined men.

"Is one of the regiments come back, Mr. Holten?" a scrawny, turkey-necked corporal inquired.

"No. It's just a little surprise we cooked up for Barryman and his scum."

"Hu ihpeya wicayapo!"

"Huka hey! Huka hey! Huka hey!"

Faces in the warehouse paled. "Holy Mary an' all the saints!" a red-faced Irish sergeant exploded. "Right what we fuckin' need. The blessed fort is under attack by the Sioux."

"Right, Sergeant Quinn. Only these are *our* Indians," Eli Holten explained. "At least, they're fighting on our side."

"Indians!" an excited voice shouted out on the walls. "We're under attack by the Sioux. Get some help up here!"

Hoofs pounded again as the Sioux began their charge. Shots rippled from the walls, answered quickly by the warriors.

"That's the signal," Holten told the noncoms. "We wait a bit and when the mutineers get out on the walls, we hit 'em in the rear."

224

"What the hell!" Howard Barryman roared. "First that idiot Strickland comes back here, now the Sioux attack us. This has to be Holten's work."

The leader of the mutiny paced back and forth across the carpets spread in General Corrington's living quarters. From outside he could hear the slow, stupefied response to the shout of alarm. Damn! Would these dolts play around until they all got their hair lifted? He strode to the door and flung it open.

"Liscomb! Get over here right away. You men, get to the wall. Send someone to move one of the cannon. Hurry your drunken ass, man!"

"There's no one who can shoot that thing, Howard," the startled mutineer protested.

"All you have to do is shove powder down the barrel, slide in a ball and ram it home, then fire it off. Goddamnit, move. Do some of your own thinking."

Vince Liscomb appeared, panting, his face alight with excitement and a tinge of fear. "There's about twenty Sioux outside. They're chargin' the north wall."

"Only the north wall? That's strange. How many men do we have up on the walls?"

"All that can make it right now."

"What do you mean, 'all who can make it'?"

"Most everyone is drunk. Some of these teamsters are there, about a dozen of our men, and a couple of the ones who only came along for the ride."

"We're going to have to do better than that. If they start riding around the fort, we'll be stretched too thin. Drag them out of their bunks if you have to. But get some men on the wall. And double the number on the north side."

"There they go," Eli told the men crowded around him. "It's time to open up."

A dozen freed noncoms poured onto the edge of the parade ground, along with the civilian volunteers. Quickly they picked out targets and opened fire. Bullets split the air, and mutineers began to fall.

"My God, they're behind us!" Butler Bell shouted. He turned, only to see a sight he had feared since the day the mutiny began. "It's the NCOs. How did they get out?"

"Who are those other fellers?"

"Don't know. Look like civilians."

A slug smacked into wood close by Bell's head and he ducked, small slivers of pine sticking in his right cheek. Behind him, beyond the palisade, the Sioux came pounding at the wall again, firing rifles as they rode. Arrows buzzed by overhead, and a few smacked into the thick pickets or vulnerable flesh. The wounded began to shriek in their misery. Bell ignored the disturbance and looked out toward the parade ground.

"That's Eli Holten down there. Goddamnit, what's going on?"

Holten ordered his platoon of noncoms and civilians forward, and they advanced. Firing all the while, their ranks were joined by the officers out of the guardhouse. Those on the walls began to fall as a hailstorm of lead crashed into them from below. Off to his right, near officers' row, Holten glimpsed movement and turned in that direction.

Vincent Liscomb steadied a Springfield, sighting on the exposed head of General Corrington. Holten's Winchester spoke sharply from his hip and splinters of clapboard flew into Liscomb's face as the bullet smashed into wood at the corner of a building. Liscomb howled as pinpricks of pain gouged his face. He turned and ran back toward the other officers' quarters. Eli started after him.

A bullet cracked through the air close to his head, and Eli whirled back to the north wall. Kneeling, Butler Bell worked the Springfield's action and chambered another round. Before he could fire, Holten brought his Winchester to his shoulder and fired a carefully aimed shot.

Scorching lead slammed into Bell's chest. He reared backward, only to catch an arrow at the base of his neck. Dead twice over, his body lurched forward, and he pitched over the lip of the parapet. Satisfied, Holten cranked the lever action and hurried after Liscomb.

Myron Henshaw stood in the doorway of Colonel Todd's quarters. Todd commanded the Ninth Regiment, now in the field, his dwelling preempted for the ambitious freebooter. Beside him stood his most trusted agent, whom he had set the task of neutralizing Eli Holten. As the fighting grew more fierce, he yelled over at Howard Barryman.

"What brought this on?"

"I don't know, but I suspect Eli Holten is behind it."

"There, you see," Henshaw snapped at his agent. "If you had kept him occupied, or killed him somehow, this would not be happening."

"Don't be too sure of that," came the brusk reply. "Holten is — a lot more than one would think."

Henshaw smiled nastily. "You should know, I suppose."

"There are too many of them. We ought to get out of here."

"The officers and noncoms have been freed. With those Indians outside, it looks pretty dark, I agree. And you're right. We should get away while we can." Myron raised his voice to call out to Howard. "Don't you think we ought to pull out? Your men are outnumbered. We've lost the supplies, damnit, but we can get away with our whole skins."

"You're right. Let me get a few things from inside."

At that moment, Vincent Liscomb came trotting toward them.

"Where are you headed?" he demanded.

"The game's up," Henshaw told him. "We're getting out while we still can."

"I'm coming along," the fiery revolutionary said flatly.

"Of course you can come," Myron soothed the fiery rabble-rouser. "We'll go after horses. You tell the men to hold fast. Once we get away, they're on their own."

"Only they ain't to know that, right?" Howard Barryman added.

Henshaw smiled nastily. "Go tell my men to start pulling back, also. Everyone to meet in the stables."

Liscomb started off to carry out instructions as Holten came trotting along officers' row. He fired another hasty shot that went astray, then he started to run. Eli took aim and squeezed off a round that smacked meatily into the thick muscle of Liscomb's left thigh.

A grunt came from the mutineer's dry throat as he twisted to his left and fell onto the solid packed dirt of the street. He rolled over and fired again at Eli, who had come closer.

Vince's bullet burned painfully across the top of Eli's shoulder. He stumbled and then jumped to the right in an attempt to get a clear shot. Liscomb had crawled behind the protection of a porch stoop. Eli studied the problem.

He had to expose himself in order to cross over and get a look at Liscomb. Meanwhile, hidden by the porch, the mutineer could work his way along the building and escape. Eli took a deep breath, chambered a round in the Winchester and darted out into the street.

Almost instantly, a Springfield barked from the direction of the porch. The slug cracked through the air uncomfortably close to Eli's head, and he dived for the ground. He executed an ungraceful forward roll and came to his knees with the Winchester at the ready.

No sign of Liscomb.

Holten didn't hesitate a second. He sprang up and ran across the street. The next shot from the Springfield came far too late.

The scout whirled and squeezed off a round the moment Liscomb's surprised face came into the field of the buckhorn rear sight.

Blood, hair, and bone sprayed from the agitator's head, and his eyes bulged as the two hundred five grain bullet destroyed his brain. Holten heard a distinctly feminine gasp a short ways down the street and glanced up in dismay.

His confusion turned to stunned immobility when he looked into the lovely blue eyes of Constance Albright. Consternation nearly cost the scout his life as Myron Henshaw drew a LeMat revolver and loosed off a bullet.

As the hammer fell, Holten jerked himself out of his paralysis and dove face first into the dirt. He rolled sideways and put the thickness of an entire house between him and Henshaw. A cold numbness filled his mind and put an ache in his heart. Somehow Connie had to be connected to this mutiny. It made him want to retch. Carefully he withdrew and sought to come at them from another direction. He rounded the corner of one officer's quarters and came face to face with Neal Thorne.

Chapter 20

His mind still occupied with the unexplained appearance of Constance Albright at Fort Rawlins, in company with men at the head of the mutiny, Eli Holten literally slammed into Neal Thorne. The two men rebounded off each other and hastily tried to put their weapons into play. Slowed by his straying thoughts, the scout lost out.

Thorne's hasty shot grazed Holten's left side, a shallow gouge that served more to knock him off his unsteady feet than to wound. Blood ran freely, and searing jangles of pain raced through his chest as he slammed solidly onto the parade ground. Surprised, Thorne stepped forward. He held his Springfield at the ready, though he had not ejected the spent cartridge nor chambered a fresh one.

"Uh — Mr. Holten. I, ah, never had anything against you. You always seemed to be fair with the men. Er — didn't mean to do that." Thorne nodded as though to indicate the wound.

"You gonna finish me off, Thorne?" the scout asked through clinched teeth.

"Uh—well, I suppose I got to, now."

"Before you do, tell me what it was that got you into this?"

"Don't suppose it will do any harm. The general had me an' Toby Whitter court-martialed and suspended on wagon wheels. All just for sneakin' a couple of drinks while we was on sentry duty. It didn't seem fair. Then, Howard, that's Howard Barryman, started talkin' about how we hadn't been given a proper trial or legal punishment. That weren't all.

"Vince Liscomb spouted a lot of nonsense about oppressed masses—whatever that means—and rising to the tide of the future. Lot of foolishness, I thought. At least until the day after me an' Toby got cut down from the punishment wheels. All of a sudden, there's this uprisin' and we controlled the fort."

"What happened next?" the scout asked in a calm voice as he started to slide his left hand toward a patch pocket on the off back side of his buckskin trousers.

"Barryman and Liscomb set themselves up in the headquarters building. Barryman took over the general's office an' Liscomb the adjutant's. They started sleepin' in the general's quarters, too. Next thing, this feller, Myron Henshaw, shows up, and we start loadin' guns and ammunition, cannon and all sorts of things into them freight wagons over there."

"Who's the woman? And how come she's here?"

"I—I don't rightly know. Her name's Constance Williams, though some of the boys who recollected her from Eagle Pass said her name there had been Albright. She's in real tight with Henshaw, that's for sure. Like they was longtime lovers."

An ache formed around Eli's heart that had nothing to do with his wounds. Visions of Connie swam in confused patterns with his brief sight of her on the porch of Colonel Todd's house, the strong arm of Myron Henshaw around her waist. While he endeavored to cover the final six inches to the pocket, he asked another question.

"Where's Whitter now?" While Thorne spoke, the scout edged his hand onto the buckle of the flap on his buckskin trousers, his fingers working to release it.

"I don't know. He took a message to Mr. Henshaw, then runned off. Least that's what Henshaw says. Reckon it's true. He didn't like the stuff Liscomb was sayin' an' how they was going to chop off the heads of the general an' all the officers. He told me once that what we did was a hanging offense."

"It is."

Thorne came in closer. "Then — then I guess we've got to kill you all, or our necks get stretched. I'm sorry, Mr. Holten. Really I am."

Neal Thorne started to raise his carbine to sight on Holten's chest. He eared back the hammer and squeezed the trigger. The weapon clicked on the expended cartridge he had not removed. Quickly he extracted it and put in another. By that time, Eli had the buckskin pouch open and delved deep within.

As Thorne brought up his Springfield, the diminutive but powerful Hammond Bull Dog .44 the scout produced from his hideout spot barked loudly. The slug smashed through Thorne's right shoulder joint and he dropped his carbine. Stumbling backward, he fought to draw his revolver left-handed. As it cleared leather, the .44 Bull Dog snarled again.

This time the sizzling bullet smacked into the hollow of Neal Thorne's throat and erupted out the back, carrying along a large fragment of a vertebra and scraps of his spinal cord.

Deprived of reliable messages, Thorne's body did a wild highland fling with the grim reaper. He jerked and twitched until the dying ex-soldier fell over and flopped like a grounded fish. Slowly, Eli Holten came to his feet and retrieved his Winchester. Then he put away the deadly little Connecticut Arms .44 and shoved replacement rounds in the tubular magazine feed well of his rifle. Howard Barryman. He'd have to look that one up next.

"We haven't time to wait for Barryman," Myron Henshaw told Constance Williams as they stood on the porch at Colonel Todd's small house.

"Besides, he's a liability," she observed coldly. "If he hadn't been so careless, none of this would have happened, and we'd be on our way to Baja California."

"So right, my dear. Though, your failure to eliminate Holten hurt us, too."

"Do you have to remind me?"

"Let's head to the stables."

Two minutes after their departure, his arms loaded with personal loot garnered from the general's quarters, Howard Barryman strained under his burden as he came out onto the porch. No sign of Henshaw or his woman. They couldn't have had too much of a head start, and they had to go to the stables. Determined not to be left behind, Barryman started down the steps and turned in the direction of the rear part of the fort.

To get there he had to cross the parade ground, round the base of the guillotine and pass through a large, double-wide gate that gave access to the stable yard and corrals. Halfway across, he heard someone shout his name.

"Barryman!" Eli Holten yelled. "Stop where you are."

Unwilling to part with his pack of valuables, Barryman speeded his pace and headed toward the wooden support posts of the execution machine. A bullet cracked a scant inch above his head and caused him to involuntarily flinch. At once, he veered his course and started for the stairs to the scaffold. He had to gain time so he could lay down his bundles and return fire.

As Barryman disappeared around the base structure of the guillotine, Holten took a desperation shot that missed. *Take him alive*, a portion of his brain yammered.

A lot of questions needed answering yet. Eli paused then to study the infernal contraption ahead of him. Everything had been made in readiness for the execution of General Corrington and Major Styles. Even the large wicker basket sat in place. The upper portion of the neck yoke had been raised in anticipation of a victim. High above, the huge weighted steel blade poised, anxious to descend and taste the rich blood of the condemned. An involuntary shudder passed over the scout as he went in pursuit of Howard Barryman.

Holten had nearly reached the scaffold when Barryman appeared above him. The mutineer had deposited his burden somewhere and now held his revolver in a steady, two-handed grip. The roar of his Colt .45 blended into the background battle sounds, though the snap of the passing chunk of lead informed Eli that Barryman had managed to fire. Before the self-appointed leader of the mutiny could manage to cock his revolver, Holten darted out of sight at the base of the terrible device.

Quickly, Holten worked his way around toward the stairs. No further opposition came from above. At the far end of the parade ground, three mutineers made a desperate dash toward the main gate. Rifle fire crackled from the freed prisoners, and the unfortunate trio went down in a heap of dust, their corpses jerking spasmodically. Gauging his chances, the scout began to climb on silent feet.

When he neared the top, he paused, then surged upward.

Howard Barryman had a chance to end all pursuit. He took quick aim and fired. A loud click sounded when the firing pin fell on a defective primer. The Colt had failed to go off. Holten was too close to allow for reloading. Barryman grasped the barrel like a tomahawk handle and swung at the scout's head.

Ducking low to avoid the powerful blow, Eli sprang forward and wrapped his arms around Barryman's legs. In an effort to retain his balance, Barryman lost his grip on his Colt. The revolver bounced harmlessly off the scout's back. Eli crawled forward and balled a fist, his aim on Barryman's jaw. The chief mutineer sharply raised one knee into Holten's already savaged scrotum. It lacked sufficient power, but even so, it elicited a low moan from Eli. The next second, Holten landed a solid punch alongside Barryman's head.

Eyes crossed and slightly glazed, Barryman fought the effects of the punch long enough to get his hand on the hilt of a large knife at his waist. He pulled it free and whipped the blade upward. The edge cleaved through buckskin and carved open flesh along the right side of the scout's rib cage.

A line of fiery pain and icy numbness followed the path of Barryman's knife. Superb reflexes saved Holten as he leaped to one side, away from the danger, and did a shoulder roll. Behind him, his enemy came to his feet and advanced once more.

Without pause to consider tactics, Holten gathered his legs under him and waited until Barryman started to raise the blood-dripping knife for a finishing plunge into his body. Then the scout leaped forward again and tackled Barryman. A cry of alarm left the murderous mutineer as he fell backward on an inclined board.

Before Holten could follow up his advantage, the locking pin popped free, and the yoke of the guillotine fell into place, securely fastening Barryman under the blade. During their struggle, Holten and Barryman had maneuvered around until they fought on the back, or executioner's side of the machine. Now the evil device firmly held Howard Barryman in its grasp. He still flailed out at the scout, though, who rolled to the side and regained his feet.

Panting, hands on hips, Eli Holten looked down at the captive Barryman. Howard's eyes bulged, and he gazed glassily upward, not at the scout but beyond to the heavy, chisel-edged blade that hung suspended over him. Oily beads of sweat popped out on the smooth forehead, and Barryman worked his mouth soundlessly. Holten walked around one of the massive uprights and bent close.

"Henshaw and Constance. Where are they headed?"

"Unnn. Eeeeaaah—I—I don't—maybe to Baja Ca-California. G-g-g-et me out of this. It—it might fall all on its own."

"What's in Baja California?"

"I don—ah, what's the use. Let me go and I'll tell you everything."

"Talk first, then we'll see."

"There is an army of freebooters waiting for the supplies Henshaw and I were to deliver from here. They plan to take the peninsula below the United States from Mexico and set up their own country."

"That sounds crazy."

"I know."

"What part does Connie have in all this?"

"She—she's an agent for Henshaw. Also his lover. She was supposed to keep you out of the way."

Holten burned with rueful disillusionment. She had been *so good* in bed. "What route will they likely take from here?"

"They never said. I—I'd guess the Santa Fe Trail partway at least. Then south into Mexico and through to California."

"Where will they be now?"

"The stables. I—was supposed to go with them."

Holten raised up. "Tell me one more thing. Would you actually have killed General Corrington?"

Naked animosity glowed in Howard's frightened eyes. "Hell yes, I would. He had too much power and I had none. I hate people like that."

Holten's hand reached out and grasped a thin lanyard.

"*No!*" Howard Barryman begged, eyes bulged in terror. "Pleeeease!"

238

Eli yanked on the cord and stepped away.

Howard Barryman continued to scream as he watched the blade descend all the way.

"So they got clean away?" Hettie Dillon asked Eli Holten a week after the battle to retake Fort Rawlins. With gentle skill, she rubbed a soothing salve along the puckered, red knife scar on his chest.

"Yes. No sign of Myron Henshaw or Constance Williams. The army telegraph alerted authorities in California, only it came to no avail. They seem to have disappeared off the earth."

"And what about you?"

"I have convalescent leave. All the time I want. With winter coming soon, there's not a lot to do at the fort. I might just stay here in Eagle Pass. The general said he would send a man here if I'm needed. I'm sore as an old grizzly and need lots of care to recover properly. That's enough about me, though. Tell me, how do you like Eagle Pass?"

"I adore it!"

"What about your excitement over the big, important school in Seattle?"

"It can run smoothly without me. Reverend Smith needs a qualified teacher to operate his school here. He asked and I said yes. The wagon train went on without me while you were at department headquarters for the court-martial of the surviving mutineers. If you want — that is, if you feel the need of a permanent, live-in nurse to care for your wounds —"

A rapid, visible swelling in the scout's loins revealed his enthusiasm for that suggestion. He reached out and pulled Hettie to him, enveloping her in his powerful arms. As he did, she reached down and began to lightly pat the bulge in his buckskin trousers.

"Hettie, Hettie, I couldn't think of a better solution to the problem. Yes, come live with me. Teach school by day and heal me by night."

Flying fingers unfastened the front of the scout's clothing and probed within for the burning member that strained for release. Humming happily, Eli conducted his own exploration of familiar terrain, cupping a petite breast and bending to kiss Hettie in the hollow of her throat.

Yes, this winter would prove to be most informative and educational, Eli Holten thought blissfully. For once he had no desire to be anywhere else.